Fictions

by **Tania Hershman**

Tangent Books

Tangent Books

First published 2012, reprint 2014
Tangent Books
Unit 5.16 Paintworks
Bristol
BS4 3EH

0117 972 0645

www.tangentbooks.co.uk

Publisher: Richard Jones
Richard@tangentbooks.co.uk

ISBN 978-1-906477-60-8

Cover Design: Joe Burt (joe@wildsparkdesign.com)
and Tom Berry (www.tomberryart.co.uk)

Typeset in Crimson by Joe Burt
Print Management: Jonathan Lewis (essentialprintmanagement@gmail.com)
Author photo © Lou Abercrombie

A CIP record for this book is available from the British Library

Printed using paper from a sustainable source.
Eco-Libris: 100 trees planted for this book.

A word about fonts

The body font used in *My Mother Was an Upright Piano* is Crimson Text, a font designed by a young German typographer called Sebastian Kosch, who now lives in Toronto where he is studying Engineering Science. Although it is a modern font, Crimson Text has classic qualities and is well suited to book production, being in the tradition of old style typefaces such as Garamound. Kosch says the font was inspired by the work of Bauhaus and Modernist typographer Jan Tschichold, Robert Slimbach who created Adobe Garamond and Jonathan Hoefler, whose best-known work is the Hoefler Text family of typefaces designed for Apple Computer which are now part of the Macintosh operating system. In 1995, Hoefler was named one of the forty most influential designers in America by *I.D. magazine*.

The heading font is IM Fell English Pro designed by Igino Marini. It's a distorted classical typeface inspired by the Fell font family designed by John Fell, who died in 1686, aged 61.

publications list

A number of these stories were previously published in the following publications:

A capella Zoo, Beat the Dust, The Binnacle 2009 Ultra-Short Contest (*My Mother Was an Upright Piano*, Grand Prize winner) Biscuit Publishing 2008 flash fiction competition, (*Vegetable, Mineral* joint winner), BRAND, Café Irreal, Contrary, Diamond Light Reading Flash Fiction Competition (*The Beam Line*, first prize), Electric Velocipede, Eleven Eleven, eyeshot, the Frogmore Papers, Ink Tears, Inky Squib, Liars' League, Litro, the London Magazine, the Los Angeles Review, Mad Hatter's Review, Metazen, Necessary Fiction, PANK magazine and the PANK 1001 Awesome Words contest, PhotoStories, Ranfurly Review, Smokelong Quarterly, Smut anthology, Southword, SPECS, Unbound Press/Spilling Ink, Vestal Review, Wellcome Collection blog, Whispered Words contest (*Ankle Socks and Hair in Bunches*, finalist).

contents

to my mother

the google 250

The Google 250. Him and 249 others. The most searched-for. So they took them into hiding. Most of them women, the famous ones, the ones you knew every curve, every smile. And him, because of his money. They flew them all to an island, somewhere, who knows where. You'll be safe here, they said. Ain't no paparazzi, ain't no-one that we don't say can come here. He breathed out.

From that day on, whenever someone with coffee-shop fever, surfing at one of those terminals, with less brain than porridge, Googled one of them, the authorities sent the Googler a warning, harshly-worded, "for your own safety". There were complaints, of course, everyone moaning, "but I need to know what he/she is…!" The authorities didn't care. This was what had to be done.

On the island, no-one was getting by very well. The most-Googled didn't know what to do with one another. People were having dreams about browser pages that had words missing, their names had wings and took flight, like heads off a goldfish. They felt like they were disappearing. He was watching one of the women, a film star, more beautiful for her proximity, all soft skin and perfect teeth. He watched her as they breakfasted together, in the communal dining room. I can see why they Googled her, he thought, over bran flakes. I would Google her too, I would Google her right now. She's got nothing to hide, he decided. But he did, now. He had something to hide called desire.

One day, after lunch prepared by that surly most-Googled British chef, he slid up behind the movie star. "I would," he whispered to her. She turned, surprised, her face frozen into annoyance at the intrusion. But then she saw him, knew him from the media, and she opened towards him. "You would...?" she said, and he saw that he was allowed to lead her by the arm back to his quarters. There, he mimed switching on the laptop he didn't have, and she shivered in anticipation. He acted out opening Google.com and she giggled; he pretended to enter her name and teased her by holding back from pressing Enter. "Do it, do it!" she cried, throwing her head back, showing him her long, pale neck. "Oh God, just do it!" He pressed Enter, she began to moan, and together they watched the phantom search results roll in.

the short tree has its hand up

The short tree has its hand up, the short tree wants to ask, wants to ask a question. The two taller trees ignore the short tree. They whisper together, the one tree leaning in to the other, giggling a little, flirting, while the short tree, its hand upraised, is crying out now.

The bridge sees the tree and wonders why it's not allowed to ask. The bridge sees the boatman and knows that the boatman will be under and through and waits for the boatman to pass. I will say something, thinks the bridge, but the house in the distance knows the bridge will never say. The house watches the bridge, for centuries now it has waited for the bridge to take courage, to speak. And not yet.

The short tree thinks about lowering its hand. The short tree thinks about giving in. It is such a day, thinks the short tree, and the clouds agree. Not a day for questions, the clouds tell the short tree. The simpering, giggling taller tree gazes into her companion. It is a day for this, thinks the giggling taller tree, not knowing that her companion is distracted. The other tall tree is paying no attention to her solicitations. The other tall tree bends and sways towards the opposite bank, where something has caught its eye. Trees have eyesight that stretches far and over, through years and through weathers, undaunted by flowing water.

The boatman has seen this all. The boatman knows the

trees. The boatman has a wife at home who doesn't like the boat at all, because she knows he loves it more than her. The boatman's boat sways a little, watching the tall trees, the short tree, the stone bridge, the stone house, and the clouds. The boat looks up at the clouds and wonders if, just if, it might be time for rain.

(inspired by painting: Le Pont de Mantes, Camille Corot)

my mother was an upright piano

My mother was an upright piano, spine erect, lid tightly closed, unplayable except by the maestro. My father was not the maestro. My father was the piano tuner; technically expert, he never made her sing. It was someone else's husband who turned her into a baby Grand.

How did I know? She told me. During the last weeks, when she was bent, lid slightly open, ivories yellowed.

"Every Tuesday," she said. "Midday. A knock at the door."

The first time, I froze. A grown woman myself, I listened to my mother talk and was back playing with dolls and wasps' nests. I cut my visit short. My mother didn't notice. She'd already fallen asleep.

The second time, I asked questions.

"Mother," I said. "He... came round. On Tuesdays. How many?"

"We are fallen stars, he said to me," whispered my mother, the formerly-upright piano. "You and me, he said. And then he would take my hand." She closed her eyes, smiled.

My father, the tuner, never took anyone's hand. He was sharp, efficient. I searched my mother's face for another hint or instruction."Should I find myself one?" I wanted to ask. "A fallen star? A maestro? Am I like you?" But she had stopped talking and begun to snore gently. I sat with her, watching the rise and fall of her chest and the way her fingers fluttered in her lap, longing for arpeggios to dance across my stiffening keys.

we will be there

I will comb your hair and when the knots have all gone, we will be there, you said to me as we lay on the floor.

Where will we be? I said, feeling as your hands started working their way, smoothing me out.

We will sail through the airport, you said. Can you see it? Close your eyes.

I did, and I could, and there was the airport, with its shops and its shopping, so many things, for every inch of space, people and things, and bags and tickets, and passports, and saying goodbyes, and making up for the most hurtful words said before the takings off and the landings. I see it, I said, and you combed and you sighed.

Shall we go to the café before the flight, you said, Shall we eat before we fly? And so we glided up escalators, trollying small cases, past dogs who were either boys or girls, I always wonder, I never know. And then in the café, one of those chains, where everything is plastic, you brought me plate after plate, I could see the colours, taste the sour-sweetness, the universal truths of food.

I'm full, I said, sitting up a little so that your comb slipped from your fingers. I looked down at you and put one hand up to feel how you had done. Are we there yet? I said, but you, retrieving the comb, didn't answer. Are we there yet? I said again, and you stood up and you looked away and I thought I had lost you. But then you sat on the sofa and you held out fingers towards me and you pulled me there too.

Let's be here, you said, and something in me twitched at your saying that.

No, I said. No. I don't want to be here, not here, not...

Ok, you said. Ok, it's alright. We're in the airplane, come lie down, and I lay at your feet, eyes tightly squeezed again, and we're there, in the air, me with the window seat, and we fly, and then land, and the country is hot and musical, rich and red and yellow.

What do we see? I said. The first thing, when we arrive?

A lion, you said, just walking around.

Just walking around? I said. As if? Just walking?

As if, you said. Living his life as if he has another life, and another one, following on from it. As if there is nothing between him and us, and everything. As if he is the largest part of the world, and the whole world is in him. We follow the lion, you said, and you hold on to his mane, and we walk with him for a long time.

Yes, I said, and I saw it, and felt the lion's mane in my hand. And I saw us walking, me and you and the lion, through the town, and out of the town, into the light and the heat and the shimmer, just me and you and the lion, walking on and on, on and on.

a loyal friend

Most people considered Jacobsen a loyal friend and so they invested everything, every cent they had. When Jacobsen failed to appear at the time they had agreed, no-one worried. Jacobsen's a friend, they said to each other. He is probably delayed, they said cheerfully, and helped themselves to nuts.

Several hours later, when attempts to contact Jacobsen had failed, they started talking in a different way. This is the point where you smile, they said to one another, and you say, We should have known. This is the point where you call the police.

Jacobsen was never found. It was never even determined where Jacobsen had come from, so to work out where he went was a lost cause. For a long time, his friends, the ones who had considered themselves confidantes and intimates, would meet and talk about him. One by one they began to confess their ignorance. What was his first name? they whispered to each other. What was he really called?

the mathematics of sunshine

It had the same effect as counting sheep does on the terminally sleepless: one neutrino, two neutrinos, four million neutrinos, and her eyes began to close. She sat up with a jerk and wiped the dribble from her mouth. Coffee. More coffee.

They called it The Hazing. Every newbie to the lab had to spend twenty–four hours calibrating the neutrino counter.

"It's vital, crucial, critical," they all assured her solemnly, as they showed her to the cavernous room and the enormous tank of liquid through which the little teeny particles streamed on their way from the sun. "It's beautiful, the mathematics of sunshine, the heart of everything. You'll never really feel what we do until you spend time with them."

And as they left her, she was sure she heard them sniggering into their lab-coated sleeves.

She knew what a neutrino was, of course she did, PhD student in particle physics. She'd been among the brightest, and here she was, suddenly, one of the lowly. Fucking neutrino babysitter. And fucking awful French vanilla fake-coffee.

She was into the twentieth hour, and the counter had ratcheted up 129,000 hits. She put her mug down and put her ear to the side of the tank. Nothing. What does a falling neutrino sound like if no-one's there to hear it? She chuckled to herself. So Zen, so Tao, she thought. So what. Okay, she'd make it through, only a few more hours, then they'd see she wasn't to be messed with.

A few minutes later, or maybe more, a loud noise woke her. The counter was spinning wildly, numbers going up and up, and the tank was vibrating, shaking. Fuck, she thought. I haven't a fucking clue what to do. It was like a washing machine out of control, an experiment going very wrong.

All her years of training suddenly drained out of her brain, and something more primal took over. Quickly, she stripped down to her underwear. "Shoes and minds left at the door," she mumbled. Then she opened the lid of the tank, the half-million-pound specially-fucking-constructed neutrino-tracking tank, and she stepped in.

The liquid was so warm, like a bath, a jacuzzi. Standing up, it reached her chest. As she stood there, the vibrations began to slow down.

"Hello," she said to no-one, or someone. And she lifted a palmful of liquid and let it drip back between her fingers. She grinned. Then she closed her eyes and threw her arms out wide. "Mathematics of fucking sunshine," she mumbled, letting herself go into the sea of invisible particles fizzing and streaming through her body.

it could almost be an accident

He meets a girl, it could almost be an accident, the way she slides into him, tips his cheek with her elbow, makes eyes at him, his whole body quivering, noticing her. It could almost be an accident, at a bus stop, or a train station, or the line for the laundrette change machine, or an ice cream vendor, or someone making fresh crêpes, the egg swirling, hardening into solid substance. It could almost be an accident but it isn't; this is what she does. She is a spy, The Devil pays her well for sliding into him, tipping his cheek with her elbow, making eyes, and she slips the cash into her bra, not trusting pockets, knowing how easy it is to finger ways inside, like electricity, and extract.

This time, her instructions were to find out how he creates it, the thing he makes so much money from, and she winds her way into his flat, into him, him inside her except it is the other way round, little does he know, as the sun streams through his rooflight, dust spinning, her cajoling, fondling, worming. She's getting inside him, into his cavities and recesses, reading his memories, his storage, and copying it for The Devil, for later. As he lies on top of her, as he plunges in and out, she half-smiles, she moans when she should, groans when she should, and all the while she is scanning him, roaming freely inside his mind, until she finds it. It is shorter than she expects, but she is not paid to judge, only to spy, and she copies it and she knows she will be well rewarded, and then she moans a little more and groans a little more, as she is supposed to, and he suspects nothing.

He makes her breakfast and he grins, shyly, and he doesn't talk about his work, he believes he is guarding himself, waiting to see if she could be the one, watching her sip her coffee, sensing what he thinks is flirting, is the beginning of something, wondering where this will go. Inside, she is folding herself closed, shutting down her probes and her scans, and when she tells him she has to go, she has to go to work, they'll fire her if she's late, and he helps her put on her coat, it could almost be an accident, letting her fingers stroke his cheek, and as she walks out into the street, she wonders why she did that, an unplanned move, not part of the exit strategy. Then she folds herself tighter inside and moves towards the subway, where she takes the express train to where The Devil is waiting for her and what she has to offer him.

trams and pies

The sticker on its smooth pink surface read "offer applies to stickered items only" and I saw that more stickers were stuck on other items, on many different things, but not on what I wanted. I wanted trams and pies. "Trams and pies, please," I asked the salesgirl and she blinked at me. "Trams and pies, please," I repeated, a little louder in case she was caught with the deafness, "and I'd like them with stickers, please, the stickers that mean that the offer applies."

"I ..I, you... you," she said, her lips rounding, and I saw she was caught with a case of the stutterings and I smiled for they say smiling unconfuses loopiness and perhaps her words would smooth out if she were smiled upon. She was sweetness, the salesgirl, and concerned for me, I could tell, wanting to assist me in my need for trams and pies. She was all concern, and she was concerned only for me, not for all the others in the shop, all the women with their small shiny handbags and the firemen and the policemen and the truckdrivers and mechanics and the boy with no hair on his head holding the hand of the ever-so-large lady with such a sweaty face I wanted to offer her handkerchiefs. No, this salesgirl had eyes only for me, as if she were the daughter, and I the mother, and she wanted to help only me, for why does a mother need a daughter if not for assistance with her daily needs, someone to set the alarm for six and make the tea for her when she wakes up, and a shoulder, when the daughter comes of age, a shoulder for the mother to weep into, and an arm to hold onto as she shuffles.

"T...trams," this unfortunate girl, whom I was beginning to view kindly as a daughter, as my child, said and her face became questioning. "Trams is not here, sorry madam. Trams is in the trams section. And pies, they're not here, we have no pies."

"No pies?" I responded cheerfully. "Why, that can't be true!" I was all encouragement and smiles, showing her my belief in her, that she would find the strength and stamina to look about her and supply my desires. "Of course you have trams and pies, just look about you, child, and you'll see it's as clear as day and night, as black and white, that I am in the correct place for them, if they are anywhere."

Another expression came over the girl's face.

"Madam," she began to say and I could see she was turning wilful, as daughters are wont to do. "Madam...," and before she could finish, I seized her sleeve and pulled her towards me. Gently, I hissed into her ear so the crowds around heard nothing.

"Trams and pies, I want, missy," I hissed, "and I thought that given what I am to you, you would have rushed to find them. If cats could sing, I'd build them myself, I am predisposed to being quite a tram- and pie-builder, but animals are mostly dumb, apart from songbirds and the like, and so I need you to help me to them."

The ungrateful wench pulled her sleeve from my grip and walked away. I stood for a moment, half believing that she was fetching me what I had asked for, but when I saw her walking, no striding, back in my direction with two large mechanics and the small bald boy, I understood that my mothering was not wanted. She was not the daughter to me and I was not the mother to her and she was striding in that way that non-daughters stride towards their non-mothers, with mechanics and bald boys, and strong words in their hands. No trams nor pies were they bringing me, no meeting of my wants and desires was going to come, and there were tables around, stickers on things on the tables, people in between the tables, and just me, with my breathing in and out, as they came to me.

I cried then for my mother, and for the trams she made me and the pies she found for me, and I cried, "Mother, come and get me!" But Mother couldn't come from the ground they had put her in, buried without her things, taking her tram-and-pie secrets into that ground. "Mother!" I cried as the mechanics came to me, one on each side, and my non-daughter was nodding her sad head up and down. I bent towards the small bald boy.

"Trams and pies?" I said into his ear on his hairless left head-side. "Bring them to me, child, and you and I will be mother and son forever, forever and four days more." And a sticker I had unstuck from an item on a table I gently slid onto his head, his shiny pink bald head, and I whispered "the offer applies, just to you and me", and waited for him to be mine.

colours shift and fade

He shouts, she shouts, the cat slinks under the sofa, the neighbour turns up the television, and finally they fall asleep.

The baby is listening from his room and wondering what all the fuss is about. He is too new to know that this is not new, this is habit. He has only been in the world for four months and it has taken him a while to overcome his wonder at the surroundings. Now that he is older he is registering events, processing them, distinguishing between his parents and others, between smells and noises and colours and where they come from. He knows that his walls are blue, and his sheets are yellow and sometimes green. He doesn't have the names of the shades, of course, but he feels the differences. He knows that the cat doesn't like him, that he musn't bite Mummy when he breast-feeds, that Daddy sometimes smells sour-ish in the mornings and that when Mummy cries he musn't join in because she cries harder and for longer and doesn't feed him.

When Daddy has gone and Mummy takes him into the kitchen, sits at the table and lifts her shirt so he can feed, he looks up into her face. He sees the dark patch around one eye shift and change, into purple then green then pink. Then one day there is a new patch, on the other side of her face, below the eye, and that changes colours too. If he touches it with his hand, Mummy twitches, says No, no, baby, and covers his fist in hers. And he knows that if he smiles at her after this, if he smiles at her any time Daddy isn't there, she will stare at him for a moment, and then slowly, slowly, her lips will move and she will do the same back to him and then she will hold him so tightly and whisper into his ear, We'll leave, next week, I'll pack and we'll go to Grandma's. Don't you worry, my love. I'm just waiting for the right time. We'll go soon. Soon. Then everything will be all right.

vegetable, mineral

I said: "Vegetable."

"Turnip?" you said.

"Nope. Ask a question."

"Are you a root vegetable?"

"No," I said. "Ask again."

"Are you in salads?" you said.

"That depends," I said.

"Depends on what?"

"On what you like to put in your salad."

I lay on the sofa, you lay on the floor, your head by my feet.

"Are you chalk?" I said.

"Chalk isn't a mineral," you said, blowing on your fingers.

"It's calcium," I said.

"So?"

"So. That's a mineral."

"No it isn't."

"Of course it is."

I got up, one of my feet slapping you on the ear as I walked over to the window.

"Do you think if we had jobs, it would be better?" you asked from the floor. I hummed something which was supposed to be "Our love will keep us warm, baby", but half way through, I couldn't remember if that was actually a song or something I'd invented.

"What?" you said.

“I’ll put the kettle on,” I said.

When you came back with the post, you held the letters out to me as if the red ink would burn through you like acid.

“Let’s run away,” I said. “Barbados, Brighton, Bermuda, Brooklyn.”

“Only B’s?” you said, and slumped onto the couch.

“Today is brought to you by the letter B,” I said.

“Animal,” you said.

“Domesticated?” I said as I shoved the bills down the back of the armchair.

“Depends,” you said.

“Depends on what?”

“If you could be bothered domesticating it.”

“Has anyone?” I said.

“What?”

“Ever domesticated it?”

“How the fuck should I know?” you said and you made movements with your hands, fluttering them in and out, that could have meant anything on any day in any country in the world.

We went out that night, you in my old jeans, me in your old tracksuit trousers, your arm through mine, five pounds in a pocket. We shared a half pint of something hopeful and sat in the corner.

“Does it eat other animals?” I said.

“Yes.”

“OK, well, that’s something.”

"Ten more questions."

I took a sip, then slid the glass towards you.

"I might do it," I said, looking out of the window at the rain hovering above the pavement.

"Don't," you said.

"I can't share half-pints and trousers with you for ever."

"OK, here's a freebie – sometimes it has a tail, sometimes it doesn't."

"It wouldn't be so bad. He wouldn't be such a nightmare boss. I mean, what worse can he do to me now that he didn't do when I was a kid?"

"The one with a tail, it can have twelve babies at a time. I mean, they're not called babies, but if I told you what they were called, that'd give it all away."

"If you sell your soul, can you buy it back later, even if it costs more?" I said, and let that hang in the air while the half-pint got warmer.

The first day, I came home and you weren't on the sofa and you weren't in the bedroom. The bathroom door was locked.

"Come out," I said. "I'm not a monster. Just a working stiff."

"Animal," you said from inside.

"Only if you come out."

"Animal." I heard you sniffle. Or it could have been a train.

"Fuck. Come on. How long have you been in there?"

"Animal."

I went to put the kettle on. When it boiled, I took our mugs and stood outside the bathroom door.

"Animal," I said.

Silence.

Finally:

"Long haired?"

"No," I said, and sat down with my back against the door. I felt you on the other side, the ridges of our spines sinking into the plywood. "Yours?"

"No."

"African?"

"Could be."

I blew on the two teas. I sucked in my breath, and thought that maybe I could hear you sucking in yours. I sat there with your mug and my mug. I imagined zebras, antelopes, wildebeest, mother lions and lion cubs. I pictured you, teaching the lion cubs party tricks, wearing my trousers.

"Domesticated?" I said, and held both mugs up to my face, watching the way the dust motes danced through the steam and twirled around in the last of the afternoon light.

graveside

Standing there, looking down and you don't believe he's gone, into the earth, when: a tap on the shoulder.

"Don't take their word for it," she says, she who did the tapping and is standing there, smart in black, smart and blonde in a suit and looking not her age, which is your age. "Mary Margaret, get down in there and see," she says, herself unlikely to climb into open graves, herself unlikely to attract even dust.

"Sylvie," you say and you know, although a stranger, she is no stranger, with her short and blonde, her smart and black.

"Not so changed, am I?" says the stranger who isn't. And the face is the same face of the time with dolls and crayons and walking through the schoolyard arm in arm, of sharing secrets and swapping stories, and crying in toilets when one hissed *Mary Margaret, how could you?* and the other wept and left. You are only smiling then and you can smile because of the terrible time it is and because of your loss and the hole, beside and inside you, and here she is not filling it and perhaps but a drop of that.

You grab her arm towards the shoulder and though you grip with the strength of ten she stands and does not shake and she is there, rock-like, for you, although years and years since the last time, minutes and hours and the universe has expanded, but it allows this now, because you need.

"You want me to say," and you look into her face, and it can't be that you don't see her hair now so short, now so unfull of the way it had been, the way it was her pride and joy and daily brushing made it so, and you with your hand on the scissors, waiting, waiting, and her sleeping, sleeping.

"Nothing," says Sylvie, who is becoming herself then, shaping up in front of you to be less than black-suited and less than smart and blonde. "Mary Margaret, I don't know about anything that wants expressing." And when she looks into you, you can stop gripping so tight and you can stop shaking yourself on the edge of the place where he is, and you step backwards once and then twice and then you turn and she follows.

Sitting in the bar, in the small room with people pressing on all sides, with people talking about him, you and she talk about other things, other times. There is grinning, and in her face you see the older, the younger. Sentences beginning with "Do you remember the time...?" And you do, how could you not?

Much later, after the hellos and goodbyes, wishing wells of people passing who pass you and have passed you all their lives and yours, Sylvie stands up.

"Margaret?" she says and you look because it's the first time.

"It is," you say.

"It fits," says she now back to looking her age, although the ghost of that long long hair still falls down her back and the ghost of your small, fat, childish fingers is touching it for the first time. "Two names is a burden, all that time it takes, all those minutes while you are saying it. Lighter, just like this."

You smile. You think about the lightness, and then with it comes the grave, again. And though you are looking at Sylvie, you are standing and peering down into it.

"Part of me," you say to her. "Part of me wants to be in there, with him."

Sylvie stays standing, doesn't reach out, doesn't touch.

"Part of you is," she says. And then, picking up her handbag, kissing you on the cheek, just a brush of the lips really, just the wing of a moth. And then: gone.

einstein plays guitar

Einstein sits in the corner, playing guitar. No-one tells him, Albert, go home. Because he's Einstein. He looks up and grins.

Einstein stands on stage, playing the violin. Everyone listens. Albert, head down, eyes closed.

Einstein plays the saxophone. The girl in the purple dress watches. She's never heard before. Of Einstein, sure, but this? Albert stands, feet wide apart, blasting.

"It's his first time," someone says. A young man, by the bar.

"In here?" says the girl in the purple dress.

"Oh no," says the young man. "First time with that." The young man moves so he can see her face.

"He's...," she says.

"Yes, we know," says the young man. He laughs. "His violin's much better. But he doesn't like to stop at that. He's not so good.... at being good. Or: just at being good. Tomorrow night it might be.... Well, who knows?"

"Isn't he a genius?" says the girl in the purple dress slowly, as if she might be tested.

The young man's shoulders twitch.

"At some things, sure," he says, pulling out a cigarette. "At some things. But he hasn't cracked this, yet." A yowl from the stage, as Albert hits a high note, far too sharp. The young man sees the girl's distraction, takes his chance, slides an arm around. "What else?" he says, inhaling.

"Oh," says the girl. "I don't know. Is there something? Else?"

"I could tell you," says the young man, who has learned a part or two about the world.

On stage, Einstein puts the instrument down, gets out a handkerchief to wipe the sweat. A woman in the crowd shouts something. Albert nods his head, smiles, picks up the sax. The girl in the purple dress follows him moving off the stage, then loses sight.

"Was that German?" she says to the young man, watching the way he smokes, like movie stars.

"Ja," says the young man and laughs and laughs as if this is the best he's ever given. He laughs so much, the girl in the purple dress inches away. The young man doesn't see. Or, if he does, he knows another trick for this.

Einstein plays the piano. The bartender unlocked it for him. Albert found the scales, trilled up, then down. The bartender washed and wiped, trying not to hear. The bartender thought instead about his wife. How she hated what he did, how he smelled of beer, cheap beer, even though he never drank.

A crash from the stage. Albert's head is on the keys. The bartender can hear him muttering to himself. Why doesn't he stick with what he knows, wonders the bartender, counting that night's change reserves.

The girl in the purple dress has brought a friend. The young man, smoking, watches them across the room. The friend annoys him, something about how she wears just red, bright screaming red. He won't speak to them, not tonight.

Einstein is warming up. Albert stands on stage, this time with his violin. He slides the bow up and down, down and up. The crowd are not yet listening, not seriously. But every single one knows who he is, why he is, and where.

When Albert starts to play, the girl in the purple dress at first hears something scratchy. But then, as she leans back, sips her orange juice, the notes come into her, as if they are a broadcast just for one.

"This is it," she murmurs, but her friend, bored, is watching a young man smoking by the bar.

On stage, Einstein moves from one melody to another, easy as light slipping between worlds. His mind is quiet. Albert plays on, watched and listened to. Even the bartender stops washing glasses, just to hear it.

dangerous shoes

"If you were a shoe you'd be designer," he said, drawing out the last word as if it would never end. "You'd be Manolo, darling, on the catwalk, teeny skinny models teetering on your precious spiky heels." She liked this image, Amazonian skeletal girls slipping Amazonian skeletal feet into her luxurious leather. Herself squat and bush-like, round-hipped and underattended, she desired someone to sauté and pour off her fat to reveal the real goddess underneath.

"Manolo," she breathed and her eyes were more glassy and lush than he had seen them in that entire first hour of acquaintance.

She reached out a squat pink finger and he wondered for a moment whether she was going to touch him and in that instant he craved her touch and also it made him feel ridiculous. What was he doing here with this pygmy woman, whose grin was a rope he wanted to tie around his slanted neck and hang. Why did they think she would suit him in any way, she who barely reaches his kneecaps, for whom he is having to utter moronic statements regarding footwear?

"My life is the sum total of the aim of my mistakes," he had told his friends, a couple fascinated by his inability to hook himself to any female for longer than it took them to decide what brand of organic coffee beans to order for the month.

"He expects to hate them all," the couple had said to each other behind his back, "and so he prepares for it and torpedoes any potential." "Let's give him something truly grotesque," they agreed, and dispatched a colleague from a neighbouring cubicle, four-foot nothing without her old-lady shoes. “See how he takes this one and destroys!” they laughed.

He sat opposite her and her finger was moving towards him and he did feel hate and he did feel revulsion, and he felt utter puzzlement when he leaned towards the digit and took it in his mouth and as he began to suck on it she breathed harder and harder, all four-foot-nothing of her, ecstasy fizzing through her veins like Coca Cola.

like owls

Someone died. That was the whisper down the line. The line that stretched, that snaked, that wound. Someone died, they hissed, pass it on. And we did, we bent towards our neighbour, our hot breath in their ear. Who, who, who? Like owls, the sounds came back. Who died, who died, who died? But nothing was returned, and no-one could see, no-one could see the front, although every day we shuffled some, we moved one foot and maybe the other. We hoped, we hoped and hoped, we clutched our numbers, shuffling.

Inside our heads we wondered if we were it, the dead, the expired. Perhaps we had all passed on but why the shuffling then? If we were dead, we thought, we'd rest. If we were dead we'd lie around all day, in sunshine if it still existed. Lucky dead, we thought, lucky not to have to queue, to eat, or breathe, or sigh, or sweat, or love or curse. Lucky, lucky, lucky.

The next day and the next, we stood, we inched, we stood. And then: a runner. A runner streaking, from behind straight up, towards the head, the start, the finish! Go go go go, we cried, clutching our numbers, our shuffling feet thrilled to the chase, thrilled to the bravery. Go go go go go! The runner vanished, far far ahead, and we strained to hear, to hear some cheers, some acts, some violence, some thing. But no, the runner's run was done. Bones broken, came the whisper, hissed from one ear to the next. Truncheons, batons, zappers, chains and stern commands. The runner won't be running now, or ever, and we giggled, laughed and cackled, foolish runner, stupid stupid stupid, no not brave, not brave. Queue we must and queue we did, no breaking free, no gaining ground.

Someone died. That was the whisper down the line. Who who who? Like owls, the sound came back.

my uncle's son

My uncle's son was a man who followed. As a boy he followed my brothers when they went out, followed as they played elaborate games, hid in caves and small spaces, shouted at him to come to the water, come jump in, come join in with them. But he, whose bones were brittle bird bones, whose hands were innocent and pale, stood to one side. My uncle's son stood, and followed.

Later on, when his bird bones had not cracked and shattered, when he had grown into an approximation of adulthood, after my uncle refused to keep him in his house, he would sit and follow. Sit in his favourite coffee shop and follow with his eyes the movements of popular girls who came in chittering and chattering, hair and smiles and nails. He sat with his drink, complaining always that it didn't taste of coffee, didn't taste of anything, watching and following the hands of the popular girls as they talked to one another, telling of last night's exploits, explaining love and life and the downsides, as they saw them, of popularity. My uncle's son, drinking his drink, wanted to soothe them, to apply language like a balm to their fruitful wounds, to give over to them the benefits of being unpopular, of being a watcher, of standing on the sidelines. But, being one himself, he had no idea how to join in, how to break in. And, besides, he was not a popular girl. They would not have listened.

I remember now a piece of night when he was with us, we were building and rebuilding new snow angels, my brothers and I, and he stood by a tree, watching, as he did. I remember that I went to him, with snow in my mittened palm, and offered it up. My uncle's son looked down at it, and at me, and in his eyes I saw that he wanted something, that he wanted what I was giving. But a muteness swallowed him and he could not accept, and I did not know then that sometimes you just need to give and keep giving until you pull the other person with you, until they are pulled over the edge and you are flying together. I think he knew that. I think that is what he was waiting for. To be pulled over, and to, finally and completely, fly.

suitcases balanced on your head

I take your words from two envelopes and I put them together, and your words, together, make something, and I am not sure what, so I stare and stare at them. Notes in cuttle ink you have given me, but mysterious, as if God is in there somewhere, waiting for me, and I can't see, I just can't see. One word: "escalator"; another word "suitcase". One travels, up and down. Another travels, too. But contains. One lifts and glides; one holds and slides. Suitcases on escalators. Escalators in suitcases. I close my eyes. I try and slip into your head, try your eyes for size. What were you seeing? What were you thinking when you scratched these out in the ink from your cuttles, and slid them into envelopes?

I have enough of sitting and thinking and trying and I get up and go into the kitchen and I see you, sitting on the counter, and you are you, you are alive-looking, and I want so much for it to be, although I know it can't, so I turn to humour to make it easy.

"Did you see Him?" I joke from a painful place in my heart, switching on the kettle. "Did you meet God at the bottom of the escalator, is that it?" But when I look at you, sitting there, your bones grown light as the sun, my window shining through your skin, you just shake your head. "Suitcases," I mumble, as the kettle boils and I feel you near me in that way

I felt you all along, all the time, ups and downs, there and not-there.

I turn sharp as nails to catch you inside a moment, I lift the kettle and make as if to splash you, threatening a ghost has become my only resort. You look as though you are going to laugh. You mouth something, but I can't hear you. It may have been, "I love you". Or maybe directions. Or a weather forecast.

I pour my tea. I turn my back on you. As if I ever could. Little conditionals and promises, that is all the stuff we were made of. And you, you couldn't even see it through. I turn my back on you and your broken promises and your future tense shattered, and I see you, at the bottom of the escalator, a suitcase balanced on your head. You are one of those Indian women, or African woman, or the ones who can carry pots, but your suitcase isn't full of water, isn't full of anything but words.

I look at your envelopes again, then I put the words back in, and one envelope inside the other and put them both on my lap. Then I begin to tear, the envelopes within envelopes, and each small part I tear off, I put in my mouth. I swallow it with tea, I rip and tear and swallow, and when I am done, when I have finished, I go into the kitchen with my mug and you have gone, but it doesn't matter anymore. I put my mug down and through the window I see what we were and where we were and I know that the rest of this life will keep on, up and down, gliding and sliding, until I, too, have had enough.

how much the ants carry

Come on, you said, skipping ahead of me. Come on! And I followed, because that's what I did then. I followed you, everywhere. I was slower, then, bigger than you, weighed down, even as a child. There was lead in my head then, clogging my thoughts, while you seemed light as a balloon, and I remember looking at you with wonder, that you didn't just raise up your arms and soar. We hid ourselves in the grass, and you would show me things, things only you knew, and I never puzzled over how it was that you had such a vast knowledge when you had spent less time on this earth than me. You were golden and glowing and I was dark, heavy and eternally grateful.

Look, you said, your nose close to the ground, watching a snake of ants doing their daily duties. Look at how hard they work, look at how much they carry. See?

I looked at the hordes and thought of my dad, going off in the morning, back late at night, nothing much to me but a grunt at breakfast and a door slamming when I was in bed already. Nothing much to me but someone there on Saturdays, slouching around the house, shouting at her, ignoring me, throwing food to the dog. And that day, that morning, for the first time, I knew what it meant to be lonely and I reached my hand toward your hair. I reached out my hand and you shook your head so it swished and tickled my nose. Then you grabbed my hand and you put it somewhere else, and, in the grass, ants scattered furiously and indignantly beneath us.

In the bar, your hair is short, almost cropped. You are the heavy one now, and I am thin from nerves, my anxiety eating away at me. I drink, and drink more and you, the seat buckling beneath your bulk, do all the talking.

They split up, you say, trying to laugh, just after we moved. They did that to us, ripped us from our home, took us half way across the country, and then she left him.

I stare at you. I try and see what you were, try and find the sunshine, but you are not just dark now, you drink in energy and I feel the space around me shrinking. You are still talking, half-crying, your hands slicing through the air as you describe the misery they heaved upon you. I can't break into this, have no solution to a one-sided conversation, so I wave to the bartender, order another round, watch your hands, your puffy face, and think about ants, shouldering twice their own body weight, marching and marching, and my hand in your hair, your golden hair. I must be smiling as I remember the grass and us, rolling, testing, growing, because you stop talking. I slide my hand over towards where your fingers are tapping on the wood, and I grip them hard. You don't make a sound, just look at me, your tiny eyes lost in your face and inside your eyes, more loss. You and I look at each other and for an instant we are back there, in those days where all there was was you leading and me following.

A glass drops, a shout, and it's gone. I release your hand, you turn away from me, and I take up my glass and wonder why it is still empty.

forty-eight dogs

In the yard were dogs. All she saw. When her husband came home from the lab she said: Look. Forty-eight dogs. Count them. Go on. Count them.He said: I see a tree. I see the grass. I don't...Dogs, she said. Forty-eight. Not fifty. There, and there, and there, and she pointed, with one hand and then the other, to all forty-eight, to the terriers and the collie, the German shepherd and the poodles. Her husband gently took her arms and turned her so that the garden, clear and quiet, was behind her. Tea, he said, seating her on the sofa.

She fiddled on the sofa arm, dug her fingers down into the cushion gaps and found a furled up twist of paper. She untwisted it and read: "Take heart, dearest. Your luck will change." She smiled at that and did take heart. The dogs, she knew, would all find homes, all forty-eight, some in pairs, some singly. The terriers and the collie, the German shepherd and the poodles.

When he came back with the tea, her husband sighed to see her softer now. He added milk and spooned in sugar and as he leant towards her with her cup, from the corner of his eye he caught the garden, shifting slightly. And in that one blink he saw it. A tail, wagging.

tiny red heart

When it sings he sings with it, him and the bird. It sings in its metal cage, with its metal wings and small metal beak, and its heart, which is part of his heart, a tiny lump that he removed from his and placed inside the bird's metal ribcage. The tiny red heart beats inside the bird and he can see it, as he stands by the cage. And when the bird sings, it fills him with joy, his bird, with his heart, his creation. And when he thinks of the day that one of them will stop singing, one of the hearts, his or the tiny bird's heart, will stop, his chest is filled with tears, sticky hot tears, that burn through him. He puts his face to the metal cage and he tells the bird, his bird, of his love and his happiness. And as the bird, the little metal bird, sings to him, he looks out of the window and he knows that one day he will have to let it go.

blue

The city was blue that night, blue all over its pavements, around its lampposts. Street signs glowed blue, people's faces were sky, their hands azure, their feet navy. No matter what anyone was wearing, it was all the same colour that night. She approached him under a lamppost, and in its blue glow she asked for the time. "Four o'clock," he said, taking her in, his eyes shifting over every blue part of her. "Dark at four o'clock," she said, looking up towards the sky and watching the clouds, lit blue by the moon. "Doesn't it worry you?" she said, without looking at him.

Later, in bed, he ran his white fingers over her white chest, the bedside light illuminating his wanderings. "I'm sorry I was...," he began, and she knew what was coming and she let her eyes slide closed so as not to see the colour of his skin when he said "it was rushed, I don't normally, first, I mean, let me apologise... I usually..." She squeezed her eyelids down and behind them saw swirling dots which she pushed together into shapes: dogs, cakes, small children with balloons. "You tore your shirt," she said, and she sat up, tossing his fingers back to him. "I'll get a needle and thread."

She watched him watching her as she sewed. "You could charge for that," he said, still looking sheepish. "A million pounds, or a thousand, or three pence a shirt, maybe." She looked up at him and the needle went into the side of her thumb. An inkspot of red blood dripped onto the shirt and she knew that she would see him again.

"I hear things," she told him after their second time, when he performed better. She knew he still found her charming and she also knew it would soon wear off, so she pulled out the big guns. "I hear lost animals who are far from their mothers. I hear shadows. I hear boots on empty streets." She was right, she could see it in his cheeks, he was taken with her. He ran a finger over her left nipple.

By the fourth encounter, she knew she was losing him. "I wrote you a poem," she said. She could see he didn't want her to read it, so she did.

"Why is my mother
Only a woman?
Why is my father
Not my father?
Should I be like all the rest?
Should I sit in a flowerpot
Amongst the insects
Inside the petals.
Let me sit
Let me sit there.
The spiders won't notice."

But it was too late, his shirt was mended, the blood dried, and his white fingers were doing up buttons, looking hungrily towards the street, the next bed, his next failure. She let him go, and stood, watching the blue night envelop him. Far away, her ears found the sound of a kitten, a spider and an angry moth. "What can I do?" she said to them, and shut the door.

life burst out

Life was small. It was tiny even, so tiny it was hard to see it sometimes. Life curled up to make itself even smaller, to fit into the kinds of holes that insects crawl into to get away from bigger insects. Life was sad. Life didn't want to be an insect. Life was getting backache from the curling up. It wanted to straighten out, stand up tall, shout out to the world. But it had been so long, Life wasn't sure how to.

I sat on the railings and looked out over the sea. Waves churned and the sun cackled from behind the clouds, and my mother, scowling, gripped the rail with both hands, her hat pulled so far down that I couldn't see her eyes.

"Do we have to...?" she said, and the wind took her words and spun them around so that they arrived jumbled. I didn't answer her anyway. She knew that yes, we did have to. So we waited.

Life started by unfurling one finger. It felt odd, stiff, unnatural. But then good, freeing, sweet. Life tried another finger, and another. A whole hand, then both. Then suddenly, like a balloon, Life burst out of itself. Life grew and grew, out of the hole and into the world and along and up and outwards.

When I saw it, I had to stop myself from grabbing my mother's arm.

"There," I hissed, and took her shoulders and turned her

towards the direction it was coming in.

"My god," my mother whispered. "I never thought I..."

We stood in silence, watching it approaching. I knew, the way I've always known about things, ever since I was little, that we were getting out of here tonight. That knowing rose up in me like holiness and light, air and fire. It lifted me out of myself.

"Come on!" I shouted and grabbed our suitcase in one hand and my mother's arm in the other, and pulled her down the steps to the beach, and we ran towards it, through the waves, my mother holding onto her hat, and the boat coming nearer and nearer.

Life bloomed and blossomed and burst through, feeling like its lungs would explode with the bursting. And finally, when it seemed to Life that it could go no further, there was a pop and a ringing sound, and everything stopped.

We were about to climb into the dinghy. I was helping my mother, she had one foot in the boot, some big guy was hauling her in, and then there was a loud noise. Everything froze. The waves iced up. The wind was gone. I couldn't move anything. But I could see it, all of it. And all I could think was, 'We were so close. So damn close. Couldn't you just let us...?'

Life looked down and saw a tiny boat with tiny people. Life couldn't remember being that small, let alone as minuscule as an insect. Now that Life was all-encompassing, Life had lost all sympathy with anything that wouldn't grow itself to

Life's stature. Life blew a little on the tiny boat. Life watched as the tiny boat swayed and tilted, dipped and dove, sank and disappeared. Then Life turned around and got on with something else.

think of icebergs

"It's hot," you said.

"Think of icebergs," I said.

"Melting," you said. "All melting. What happens?"

"When?"

"When we run out of ice?"

I put my arm around you, felt your bony shoulders.

"Don't worry," I said. "People are clever. Very clever. There'll always be freezers. And iced coffee."

We spent the sweltering summer wearing very little and standing very still in the dark corners of your dust-filled flat. I traced the sweat sliding down your thin arms, you wiped my forehead with a towel as if I were your poor, dying Victorian husband.

When things got unbearable, our refuge was the lobby of the Grand. We sat, our long bare legs curled up beneath us, sipping iced coffees and bathing in the freezing air. We watched businessmen in heavy suits flock together and swoop into the dining room, and ladies with small dogs, high hairdos and large luggage being escorted to the lifts.

"Heaven," you said, slurping your iced-coffee-flavoured foam. "Paradise."

But when we revolved out of the doors, it was worse than ever. A sizzling frying pan to the face.

"Hell," you said. "We're taking the Fire Line straight to the Inferno."

You tipped your head back and looked up at the blue-perfect, dazzling sky.

"I think ...it might rain," you said.

"That's what I've heard," I said. Both of us, standing on the melting pavement, heads tipped back, pools of salty sweat running down into our aching, dry eyes.

it's the state I'm in

Instead of the cod, she chose the fin.

"Why?" said Leonard, lifting his beer glass and looking at her through the foam.

"It's the state I'm in," she said. "I'm in that place. It's all fins for me from now on."

"You know what they say," Leonard said, tilting his beer glass slightly. She pictured beer and tabletop meeting. She held her breath. He put the glass down. "Down with the sharks, better to face the fin in the water."

"Who says that?" She couldn't take her eyes off Leonard's beer glass as if it would somehow begin dancing or doing something else ludicrous and vital that if she looked away she would miss.

"Up here," said Leonard, and he put his arm protectively around his beer. "No coveting a man's beverage, madam."

"Sorry," she said. "Better to face the fin? Well, we'll see."

"In your case, better the fin lightly sautéed in garlic butter," and as he said that she saw the fin, perhaps with a shark attached, swimming around in her kitchen sink. And she saw herself noticing the fin, walking back towards the kitchen when the intercom buzzes, and the fin stops circling and the buzzing gets louder.

"Come on," said Leonard. "Pretend I'm your Oracle, I'm the Sage of Palmers Green. If you listen to what I say it will all be alright."

She looked him in the eye.

"Shoot," she said. Leonard pretend to rack his brains.

"Alright," he said after a few moments of pantomime sagery. "Here it is. Wait for it. There are only choices, one thing and then another, yes or no."

"Oh," she said.

"Does that...?" Leonard said, leaning back and holding up his glass again to look through the foam at the fluorescent ceiling light.

"I don't know. Maybe. If I'm lucky. If I'm lucky I'll know when to say yes and when to say no."

"We are all lucky," Leonard said. "That's it. The Oracle has spoken. I'm going to the loo." He got up. "Don't touch my beer."

"Ok," she said, and as she watched Leonard weave through the tables she imagined him with a fin, she imagined him in her kitchen sink, circling and circling, as the buzzer buzzed and buzzed and she just stood there, not knowing which way to turn.

underground

We took the board down to the track and sat in the tunnel. We chose a Banker, who gave out the money, by torchlight, and we took one each: iron, shoe, top hat, Scottie dog. The wind danced, watching us as we made our way around, past Mayfair and Piccadilly Circus, Bond Street and the Electric Company. No-one said, Isn't it funny that we're underneath...? No-one said, Everyone above, if only they knew... We sat there, rolling the dice, buying houses, hotels, paying fines, winning beauty contests, in the darkness, rumblings all around us.

The talk turned at some point to the question of questions. Some of us argued in favour, that interrogatory thinking is the basis for intellectual evolution; some that querying anything was a loss of valuable time, because there are no answers.

"What about physics?" said those of us who were in favour. "We wouldn't have split the atom, discovered quarks, dark matter, black holes," as the tunnel shuddered in the night's grip, our torchlight sputtering and quaking.

"We're not happier now than we were before atoms were split, before Steven Hawking, before the Big Bang," said those of us against, who refused even to end their remarks with a questioning tone.

"Who says?" asked those of us in favour.

"Disprove it," declared those of us against.

Someone picked up a Community Chest card. "Everyone must donate 10 percent of his holdings to you in cash."

"Why the fuck should we?"

"There are rules."

"Fuck that."

Someone tipped up the board, hotels went flying, pink, green and blue money fluttered down the tracks, the iron and the Scottie dog, the shoe and the top hat fell, one clanging after another, metal on metal.

"See what happens with questions," declared those of us against.

"Is your way any better?" asked those of us in favour. Banker started picking it all up, and we scattered to retrieve the parts and return them to the box. Those in favour of questions wondered to themselves why we bothered coming down here, and those against told themselves this was a stupid idea to begin with.

The train appeared faster than we expected. One moment: darkness; the next, dazzle. We stood, flattening ourselves against the wall as it burst past us, crushing houses, hotels, famous London streets. The power of the hulking machine trembled and shook our bones and our hearts split apart and rejoined, singing to the thundering of the wheels.

Afterwards, we picked up the board, put it back in the box, closed the lid, and walked, slowly and in silence, out of the tunnel and back up into the light.

manoeuvres

I don't understand it, she said, knowing that somewhere, in some country, rockets were falling, bloody world, getting bloodier. She looked at you and she said that. I don't understand it. And you were supposed to? You were supposed to explain it? With your sagging cappucino and your sad hands and your small face?

Me? you said, and you hoped she might return your fire with explanations of her own, but she looked down and down into her tea as if your answer was the single greatest disappointment of her life.

In bed later, there was a silence between you and her. You had been allowed to touch, with your sad hands and your small face and your dry lips, and she touched you too and it was mutual, you hoped, the feeling inside your belly. It was a whimper of a feeling, nothing explosive, just a possible spark-to-be, surounded by your particular brand of defenses, walls and armed guards. You wondered whether it would grow, whether it would be allowed, while your armed guards paced up and down beside it, around it and around its fortifications.

I don't understand it either, you whispered into her ear, and inside you something lit up.

Later, when the big guns had come out, when you and she had made declarations and parties were amassing, she watched the news.

Look, she said as she scanned the parade of burned faces and torched cities. Look, and she pulled you so hard down towards her you thought she might snap you. She made you watch it with her, but from the side you were watching her, the way her skin shivered as the minutes passed, her eyes flicking from one thing to another, jumping and startled. You wanted to say something about destroying the television, about creating a sanctuary, but the words wouldn't come out. You held still.

Over the years, she flared up less often, dulled by the infinite parade of catastrophe. You observed her as each day ended with the nightly broadcast, waiting for eruptions, planning your strategy, but they become less and less. Her surrender was such that, when the television, a replacement of the original, finally expired, she raised no objection to leaving its spot unfilled.

She turned to jigsaws, remembering a childhood passion, spread them out on the dining table and plotted their construction as a general planning manoeuvres. You were calmer too, then, as the images appeared: church scenes, flowers, complicated paintings which she furiously assembled.

When she finished, when order was restored, she sat on the sofa, holding your hand, her face alight with accomplishment, her tired eyelids falling, and outside the moon completed the world, quiet as it was in your own small corner.

disease relics

There is an office with a sign that reads

Disease relics.

Inside this office there are assorted ones. Such as the one with peyote buttons for eyes. She is sour and demanding, shouting and tut-tutting. And the one with a mobile phone for a mouth, who is silent. The assorted ones sort through the relics, what got left behind when.

I was there then, busy, learning how to graft. I had my parts then, when I started. But some time passed and then my small finger on the left hand, just that one, became a slice of sock. It didn't hinder. I could make do, just fine. My job there was to sift the flakes, all sizes there, from blanched moths up to carpets, some. Gloves we wore always, special ones, and then fitting my finger in was odd. But in the end it worked.

Each flake would have a label, stating facts like time and year and succumbment ratio. All the label colours were for me to make. At first I stayed with cream and white and yellow, then, when I was feeling fiery it was orange-red, but lately I've a deep desire for blues and greens. No-one comes and stares with her peyote eyes or mobile mouth, so I just do it.

But then she did come, she with ears of car tires, and I thought she came to whip me, but she came to cry. She came to say how she loved. The man she loved, he was a singer. Oh how she wanted him and only him and went each night to be there. But he could not. You see why.

The tires.

Oh shame. I listened as I labelled flake and flake and once I wanted just to touch her. But we can't. Gloves on, always gloves, and such thick thick ones. So I stuck with seeing her and hearing her and hoped that it might help.

The day she didn't come, no-one explained. She'd gone and in her spot another sat, with all her parts, so far. And I felt something shift and there, my knee, which once was fine, was now a hairbrush. What could I do but sigh and then go back to work?

we keep the wall between us as we go

It was Valerie's idea. Just a little one, she said. One we can carry around with us. Doesn't have to be that high. We need to be able to see over it in case of emergency. And it can't be too heavy, something light, some kind of aluminium brick, she suggested. I'd never heard of aluminium bricks. I thought that maybe the space shuttle was made of them, so it can get back in through the atmosphere. I said that and on Valerie's face I could see clearly that she thought I was an idiot (hadn't Mother always thought so too?) but she decided to humour me.

We went to the DIY store.

"We need a portable wall," my sister said to the young man in the red overalls. He thought for a moment.

"Well, I s'pose this could be portable," he said, ushering us to Fencing. Valerie lifted up a light bamboo section.

"What do you think?" she said to me, but I could see her mind was made up.

Now we have it between us at breakfast, lunch and dinner. Valerie says,

"Pass the potatoes,"

and I reach over the wall/fence to hand them to her.

"Thank you," she says.

Valerie insists we take it when we go out, too. She says we can take turns carrying it, but I think that because it's her idea, she should shoulder most of the burden. This doesn't go down well. She glares at me, her face, which is so like my face and at the same time so completely different, folds into little creases of disappointment at the fact that I don't think like her, don't understand what she's getting at.

"Ok, ok," I say, and I pick up the wall/fence, which is hard to hold onto, bamboo being kind of slippery, and I take it out of the door. Valerie's face relaxes.

"Off we go!" she says and if she wasn't so almost-elderly I'd think she was about to skip.

In the tea rooms we meet Sandra and Jacqueline. They like the wall idea.

"It's just so unique," says Sandra, who always favoured Valerie, always tried to get in her good books. "Separation, yet togetherness. Two, yet one." Valerie beams. Sandra understands, Valerie's grin says. Sandra may not be my blood relation, says Valerie's beaming smile, but she knows me.

"It's moveable art," says Jacqueline, who lives in another world most of the time, and she gazes at the bamboo as if she wants to eat it.

I sigh, and everyone ignores me. I lift up my tea cup, blow on it, think to say something, know that it will be roundly dismissed, and take a sip of tea instead.

I think about aluminium bricks.

I think about a taller wall, a wall that would block out Valerie's smarmy face, her aggravating laugh, her screechy voice.

And I wonder if, when she isn't looking, I could crouch down behind the wall/fence and slip quietly away.

that small small inch

You thought it was the oddest setting. You thought it was the strangest place to meet: a phone box. I said, I am very fond of this one. You looked at me like that again. Don't look at me like that, I said back to you, my nose an inch from yours inside this joyful phone box. I did grin then, to demonstrate that this was fun, a date. You didn't grin right back, as if you thought, Oh no, one of these spirits has gone inside her, what will she do now and next and after that and me here just a small small inch away? I heard you think that, really I did, we were pressing stomach to stomach. Feel it! I said to you then, and then my hunger made itself too clear. You did smile then and reached your hand across that inch and put it on my tummy. Does your phone box have coffee or cake? you said then, but your fingers on my cardigan which was only millimetres from the skin below had sent me flapping, all of me, and every warmth a spark a burst of red delight that I could no longer talk. I looked it into you instead, looked my words into your eyes and then, oh then, you heard it clear and crossed that small small inch once more, this time with your mouth.

a pigeon and a sparrow

Levin was bothered by the pigeons in a different way from the way he was bothered by the sparrows, and again this differed from his discomfort at robins and his distaste for owls, especially barn owls. Should you mention to him a larger bird, an eagle, perhaps, or a vulture, you would see the shudder that played him like a piano. And you might ask him what exactly the problem was, or you might ask him why not a similar disaffection for all birds. You might ask this but you would see only the side of Levin's head as he walked away to find someone whose conversation was more conducive to his moods, his repulsions.

You might then turn to someone else, that red-headed woman in the corner you caught staring earlier, while you were speaking to Levin, and ask her. Don't, she might say, don't get caught in that snare, you'll flail like a rabbit and you'll never tear free, and then she might ask you to refill her drink and while you do it you wonder why you ever agreed to come at all.

At home later, when you are assessing how the night's interactions went, you see Levin again, you hear his voice and you think to yourself, I should have been more gentle. I should have been kinder, you think. And when you turn off your bedside light, you see a pigeon and a sparrow on a branch. And they stare at each other until the sun goes down and the stars come out.

waving on the moon

"They're waving at us," said Jorg. Morten peered at the grainy screen. She thought she might be able to see someone's arm moving.

"How do they know we're here?" said Jorg.

"Well, we are quite a large probe, if they've got the right scope," said Morten. "Or maybe they wave at everyone?"

Instead of carrying on the conversation, they went into Morten's pod, had sex, and then Jorg went off to paint his toy soldiers, or whatever it was that he did, Morten wasn't sure, even after nine years. She went back to sit at the console. Yes, it did look like someone waving. She tried to slide in closer, but something about the atmosphere on this particular moon held them back.

She wished she could wave.

She waved anyway.

Then she felt stupid so she fiddled with her hair as if that was what she'd always meant to do. She looked around to see if Jorg was there. I'm an idiot, she thought, and decided to reassess their transit logs, just to pass the time.

In his room, Jorg was painting toy soldiers. He had spent almost a decade working on this regiment. He was nearly done and as he sat with his fine brush, filling in the khaki of the officer's uniform, he wondered what he might do next. He wondered if Morten would want to see them. He wondered if she might laugh at the whole thing. Nine years on this mission and he really wasn't sure at any given moment what she might do.

"What do you think?" he said to the soldier, standing him on the desk. Then he remembered it was a Russian regiment. He didn't speak Russian. He dipped the paintbrush back in the khaki and picked up the soldier.

On the moon, someone was waving. They waved a lot, to exercise their arms. And also, just in case. The waver wasn't sure if anyone was passing, at any given moment. The waver didn't know, because it had been so long since the stranding, whether technology had reached a point where this moon's surface might be seen from far far far away. It had been so long since the stranding that the waver wasn't sure even about self, what self might be, a he or she or an other, the waver had forgotten it all. But not how to wave. That still remained.

On another moon, a couple stood, drinking cocktails.

"Someone's waving over there, I think," said he, who had implants to enable vision farzoom if required, as well as microscopic.

"How nice, dear," said she, who was a little tipsy already, although she had been secretly practising in the afternoons, raising her tolerance, feeling a little foolish at how quickly she wobbled.

"I'll wave back, shall I?" he said, handing her the glass. He raised his right arm. "Ahoy there!" and she, holding both glasses, looked around at their moon and sighed, because really, did life get any better than this?

transparent

I can see through her. She is sitting opposite me and I see her ribs, the blood beating in her heart, the tea as it makes its way down towards her stomach. Yesterday we were sitting here as couples do, cut off from one another by skin, by outward defenses. Today, she is as open to me as my own mind.

"Can you...?" I say, my eyes fixed to her thin frame, watching the brown liquid slide down her throat, seeing her lungs fill with air.

"Milk?" she says, passing it over. She cannot see through me, clearly. This is one way only.

"Are you...?" I say, and I hold my breath in case this should all disappear, in case her flesh should instantly return, clouding the vision. I want to say, Are you feeling alright? She looks at me.

"What's wrong with you?" she says, and her tone is usual, normal, the tone of someone who does not know that their lover can see straight into their colon, the twists and turns of their intestines. I force my eyes up to her face, and I see her sinuses, the roots of her teeth, and I gasp. She puts down her mug and stands and comes over to me and puts a hand of bones on my forehead and bends down to me, pressing her veined cheek to my skin.

"I think you're feverish," she says, and she goes to find our thermometer, and I watch her spine shift and elongate and compress as she bends down to rummage through drawers and I wait for her cool hand on my hot face and wonder whether she can see through me anyway.

in triplicate

Due to a person under a train it shan't be me today. Someone's already done it, I hear on the radio. I'd planned it carefully, writing it out in triplicate on carbon paper, but had included a clause. For occasions such as this. I was to be the only one, as far as possible measures could ensure it. Just me, the train tracks, and whatever happened between us. Where are my triplicate copies, here they are and here is where I signed and here's that clause and here's me going back to bed again, in go the ear plugs.

It takes so long to re-prepare the paperwork, these things musn't be rushed, and always in triplicate, carbon paper, that it is a month before the day comes up again. The news is clear, only the seeds of more conflict growing in some far off place, not near me, not near the train tracks, and whatever happens between us. I fill in the appropriate sections, stack the papers on my small table, tidily straightened, and leave the house in what I'd decided to wear.

Standing on the platform of my chosen station, I smell a smell that smells like plasticine and all of a flash I see in my mind's eye my papers blow away. I see my small table, all messed up, no-one now would understand the plan, my intentions gone, all gone, and so I have to leave. I have to rush back home to check, and all from the smell of plasticine which I don't remember meaning much to me. I don't remember much of that at all so maybe it did. It might have been everything back then and that is why.

The papers are perfectly there, of course, but now the plan is ruined. So it shan't be me today. I shred the papers as before and lie back in my bed to plan again. These things take time, they can't be rushed. And always in triplicate.

move quickly now

She said, "Move quickly now and we'll go together. No, don't look behind. No, don't." He wondered but followed, only being small and not yet ready for disagreements. Or, rather, not yet ready to see if this would be what he decided to be disagreeable about. He was a small boy who chose his battles carefully, understanding almost from the first moment that it was not worthwhile to waste his energies. So he had sat, a calm and fat baby, watching and assessing. She had expected more cries, more shrieking, and was relieved when he turned out not to be one of those. She had shown him off to friends.

"He's placid, so placid," said her friends, ragged around their eyes and mouths from bewildered and uncalm nights with their own. They looked at him greedily and soon she stopped seeing those sorts of friends, those sorts of mothers.

They walked together along the road, but he wanted to look back. She held his hand as if gripping onto a rope ladder dangling over a gorge. Gripped him so tightly.

"How do you know where we'll get to?" he said, and she wanted to say something original, something about crystal balls or divination by means of arrows, but she was tired and he was too clever, so she said:

"I have a map, and I've got an address for us. Don't worry."

"I'm not worried," said the boy, and he wasn't, but he was curious.

They came across the first body some hours later, as she moved them both off the road to rest between trees. She stopped still, and he stood behind her and for one quick instant she wished she could fly, to just take him and go up and up and never have to show him anything but clouds again.

He stared at the body, which had wounds to its head. Probably caused by a knife, thought the boy, without thinking how he might possibly know that. She was staring at the face, which had a faraway look to it.

They stood there for a long time, the woman and the boy and the dead man. He had the word "father" circling in his mind, and she was trying not to cry, not to just sit there and raise her arms up to the world and the circling crows.

"Come on," said the boy, and he took her hand. "Come on, let's go," and he led her away and back to the road, and they carried on walking.

if

If we meet up, years from now, in a café, say. If we sit there, in a café, you and me, how will it be? Will it be as though you never held me at all? Will it be as though your skin doesn't know my skin?

You're lying in my bed, and I'm sitting up and looking at the wall, the one with the mirror. I can see myself in the mirror, and the edge of you, an elbow, maybe. I am looking at myself and wondering if I am different now, after we've been together, after we've shared and rolled and touched and released. I am trying to see something in me, and you're breathing heavily, and then your hand is on my back.

"What are you doing?"

"Nothing, go back to sleep."

"I'm not sleeping."

If we meet years from now, in a restaurant, will I tell you about that moment? Will you ask me, ask me again, what was I doing? Or will it all have flown away on our breath, the mingled molecules dancing over an ocean across the other side of the world?

I'm lying in your bed. You're sitting up, your back to me, naked.

"Sorry," you say to me without turning round.

"Love means never," I start to say, and then stop, something pulling me back, a voice, a voice of reason, that I forgot I had. Or a voice of reason coming to me from somewhere else, some other time. The voice said, "Untrue. Untrue. Sorry. He's sorry. He will be."

"Love," you say without turning round and that's when I hear it. I hear then the echo of what you will say to me years later. Years later, when we meet, in a bar, a dark bar, darkness closing you off from me, hiding my ageing from you.

"Why here?" I will ask you and you will say something about this being your favourite, this being the place they all know you, or where they mix what you need them to mix in the way that you need it. You will sound harder, then. I will remember your back, naked, as I lay on your bed.

"Love," you will say. "Love destroyed everything for me."

"Our love?" I will ask, although that voice will tell me that I already know. You won't answer. You will just hide your face from me in the darkness, drink your well-mixed drink, and I will slide away from you, millimetre by millimetre, until I am not in that bar, that café, that restaurant. Until I am not in that year at all, and we never meet again.

at camden town he said he loved me

We shared an armrest on the Northern Line, our elbows sidling into one another. He said he was a poet. He said he loved me even before we got to Camden Town. By Chalk Farm, he offered eternal devotion.

"Don't rush me," I said. "I'll give you my answer at Charing Cross."

He waited, scratched his nose. I looked him up and down, through tunnels and at station stops, and wondered if he'd just be one more heart-shaped bruise on my already-mottled skin.

I got out early, slid through the doors at King's Cross just before they shut, and stood there, watching him paw at the window with his poet's fingers, confusion in his eyes. I thought he mouthed, *I love you,* but it could have been, *You're just another emotional virgin.* I rode up the escalator wondering how it might have been, but by the time I'd crossed over to the Victoria line, I was already scanning the platform, hoping that here I'd find my true love.

the painter and the physicist

The curtain is pulled back.

Yes? Says the assistant.

I've come... to see. To see the painter.

And you are...?

I... I'm the physicist.

One moment, says the assistant and the curtain falls back again.

The painter doesn't turn round.

Send the physicist in, says the painter, cleaning a brush.

The physicist sits on a stool, watching as the painter chooses colours.

So, says the painter, you're a physicist.

Yes, I... Theoretical physics.

Unseen. You imagine what's there.

The physicist is uncomfortable, shifting a little, the stool leg rocking. The painter is mixing two colours on the palette. The physicist watches the painter and wonders how it works, what the eye sees, what the eye knows.

I suppose, says the physicist. Yes, that is certainly one way to put it. Some might say we, umm, guess. We are just guessers. I mean, well, educated guessers! The physicist laughs, shortly, quickly.

Electrons, says the painter. What do you think an electron looks like?

Looks like? An electron?

Does it have colour? says the painter, licking the tip of the paintbrush.

I... I don't...

Don't think, says the painter.

Blue, says the physicist, who doesn't see the painter grinning.

Blue. A blue electron.

Yes, says the physicist, whose mind is trying to ask what the relevance of this can possibly be to current research projects. Cobalt, says the physicist, unsure exactly what shade this is. Or azure.

Cobalt, or azure. Very specific, says the painter. Wavelengths make all the difference, don't they.

Yes! says the physicist, who almost falls off the stool. The way a colour hits the eye. I mean.. I'm not a biologist, of course, I'm not familiar with the structure, the rods and the cones and...

Neutron, would that be white, says the painter, who has now added several brushstrokes to the canvas.

Well, I suppose so, although now that you ask, I imagine them more as, well, grey. The physicist looks at the canvas and wonders if a question would be appropriate at this point. Your painting, says the physicist quietly.

You want to know if I know what it is going to look like, says the painter.

You don't have to... please don't feel you, I mean, I just came to.. It's your..

There is something, says the painter, turning away from the canvas and towards the stool where the physicist, uncomfortable again, is fidgeting. The painter holds up the brush and then holds it out. Something. I can see it out of the corner of my eye, a hint of it. But, if I try and look at it directly, it vanishes. I have to move towards it...

Slowly, yes, says the physicist. Like a small animal, or a child. So you don't...

Scare it, says the painter. The painter smiles again, still facing the physicist. Theories, says the painter. For you, too?

Yes, says the physicist, who hasn't thought about falling off the stool for quite some time now.

Later, when the canvas is half-covered, the painter puts the brushes down and suggests they go for a drink. In the pub corner, the physicist has a single malt, the painter a glass of dry red. The painter picks up the physicist's glass and holds it to the light.

Look at that, says the painter. The shades of gold.

The way the photons hit the liquid, some are reflected, some pass through.

It shimmers, says the painter. Hard to capture that, hard to express the movement, the angles, the flow.

I could, says the physicist, tell you about flow, give you equations, write it down on a napkin.

Xs and ys, says the painter, grimacing.

Hey, says the physicist, tongue loosened. Those are *my* colours.

What colour is an X? says the painter, sipping the dry red, thinking of ochre, scarlet, black.

Green, says the physicist, who has never imagined it before, but now, once the word emerges, sees it all over the blackboards, the whiteboards, the pages of notebooks.

And if I said to you, X must be pink, says the painter.

No, says the physicist. Wrong.

Aha! says the painter.

Oh, says the physicist, and grins. I see. And if I said to you, paint the sky brown...

It's been done, says the painter, who doesn't like to be predictable. The physicist nudges the painter's elbow and then wonders where the boldness comes from.

Are you telling me, says the physicist, that there is no wrong?

Oh, says the painter. I don't... well. I couldn't. I mean...

Aha! says the physicist, getting up. Another round?

The next day, the painter paints; the physicist teaches a class. The day after that, they sit together again, in the pub. The following week, the painter visits the physicist. In the space between them, colours flow.

into the waiting arms of god

Flamenco Bob stood me on his lap and the crowd went wild.

"See this child!" he cried. "See her? See her?"

"Yes!" they shouted and their shouts shuddered through me, so thin was I, and wearing only the flowing robes that Flamenco Bob thought to put me in. "We see her!" and I felt all their eyes upon me and all their hopes were upon me to and the weight of it all was enough to shake me and shiver me. Bob tightened his hold upon my ankles and I heard a whisper from him.

"Be strong for me," he hissed and his fingers dug into my skin and I knew I could do it, I could be strong. And I threw my arms up in the air and there was cheering and stamping and Flamenco Bob's hot breathing was upon my back and he was crying those tears and he was telling them to pray and about the seven ways to get to heaven, and he was saying, You can do it, yes you can, such is your human love, and I was bathing in it all and I could have stayed there for ever.

When it was all over, when the crowd had departed and I was allowed to descend and I stood on the ground, Bob put his hands to my face, upon my cheeks reddened from all the excitement.

"You are my own angel," he said, and "You are the Way, the Path, and they can feel it," and "I will never leave you, it is you and I for ever," and I gazed into Flamenco Bob's eyes and I knew that what he was saying was true and that I was the one he would pick for his wife, I over all the others, and together we would ascend, together, he and I, into the waiting arms of God.

containing art

We just love Art in containers, any sort of glass jars, or Tupperware, even. We adore that sense of containment, the feeling that the Art isn't going to, well, leak out. Or that something else will get into the Art. Art contamination, it's something we worry about a great deal. Some Art, it's terribly sensitive, you know. It's fragile, like a baby, or more like a soufflé. The smallest thing can deflate it, like tapping a balloon with a sharp pin. We know about fallen soufflés, we are all familiar with that utterly crushing sense of failure, that sudden destruction of all hope, as we gazed upon our Creation, sinking, sinking.

We don't want that to happen to Art.

So we prefer Art when it's protected. A frame doesn't do it. We debated this for a while but came to the unanimous conclusion that frames are simply not enough. A Painting must be encased, preferably hermetically sealed. There are ways of doing it so that you can still see the Painting, of course. We wouldn't want that, Art must be looked at and adored. We did some research and we're satisfied that there are ways.

Sculptures, especially the little ones, work very well in Tupperware. Tupperware comes in so many shapes, it's so versatile, we all know that from our own collections. It has that Lifetime Guarantee as well, so you never have to worry.

We have a few early Rodin pieces in different Tupperware containers right now, and we all agree, it doesn't diminish their beauty one bit.

Of course, Modern Art, the Damien-Hurst-Let's-Kill-A-Kitten school, must be contained, what with all that blood and other liquid. He's so very good at that. We've had several discussions just about him and his mastery of the containment. We thought about inviting him, perhaps, to lecture on it. When he's not busy, creating, of course. One of us knows someone who knows someone who knows his friend's wife's brother. And someone else knows a journalist who could perhaps write about the visit and the lecture. That's important to us. We feel that this subject needs a wider audience. We'd love more participation in this discussion. We would be open to new types of containers, new technologies, new sealing methods. We're a very open-minded group. We're just concerned, and we simply love Art.

the family

Although the family is not always available, the family is on hand when it comes to death. The family stands a respectful distance away, swaying slightly as the coffin is lowered, every now and then blowing a nose. Back at the house, the family are convivial, shaking hands, patting backs, handing food around. The family are good like that. In the pandemonium that is mothers and children, fathers and whisky, small dogs and the one that cries a lot under a table, the family takes charge, ushers and whisks, cajoles and sweeps away.

The family is especially on hand for those medium-sized boys with their exploding watches, exploding eggs, exploding matches, whom the family, in formation, scoops up before damage is done so that grieving can continue. And when it is over, the family clears away the necessary before making a quiet exit.

After that, the family may not be available, may be unseen and unheard from for months or perhaps even years. When people ask you a question about the family, answer them vaguely, for the family do not like to be proscribed, assigned to boxes, dates, labels. When they come, they come. And don't forget your manners.

the apple trees watched and wondered

Once, an angry man dragged his father along the ground through his own orchard. An apple tree watched and wondered, watched and wondered, as the angry man, his father's feet in his hands, heaving, sweating, and the father of the angry man, his arms up towards some kind of heaven, moaned and sobbed. The apple tree asked the tree next to her for an explanation, and the whisper circulated the orchard but no-one knew, no-one understood. Apple trees do not know anger, but they do know fathers, and they do know sons. They know that one comes from the other, one is like the other but different, similar and unique. Apple trees keep a certain distance, one from the next, to preserve this, similar, unique. The apple trees watched as the angry man dragged and heaved and the father moaned and sobbed, and then, by the edge of the orchard, near the high hedge past which the apple trees could see horses gently eating, the angry man beat and pummelled and the father screamed and groaned and the wind held the screams and groans and the apple trees could hear them then and afterwards, for a long time afterwards, and for a long time after, all the apples in the orchard were sour and angry and brown and purple and fell to the ground and rolled away into the mud.

under the tree

Under the tree
He sits and I come out and I bring him breakfastlunchdinner, and he says, I'm fine Mum, don't worry Mum, but he doesn't get up, doesn't come in. Just sits, under the tree. And I sit, in the kitchen, opposite the window, and watch him. Then, when it's too dark to see anymore, I stumble upstairs, fall onto the bed. The next morning I get up and we do it all again.

First day
I was curious, puzzled, asked him in a jokey way, Are you trying out for the local drama club, is that it? Make a great plant, you would, I say, trying for a laugh, for a fightback, for a getting-up-standing-up-stopping-all-this-nonsense. But what I got was a grin, a nod, nothing at all, no answers, all open, everything hanging, falling apart.

Second day
My stomach's knotting itself, whispering words, not-normal-you've-always-known-it-better-call-someone words, burning words, and I'm trying to be Regular Mum, carrying out breakfastlunchdinner on trays, with folded napkins, Jokey Mum sounding thin, worry creeping in, urges to slap and shake just under my upmost thoughts. Get up, get up, but I don't say it, I'm humouring him humouring me, him in the same clothes as two days ago, in the same spot, but looking fine, teenagery, smiling. What would I say to someone, what

would I say? Coming in? I ask like I was just tossing it out there, like it wasn't important, like I didn't want to get a bulldozer and dig up that tree, digupthewholegarden just to get him inside. It's peaceful, he says. Right here, he says, looking up through the branches, up at something, and I'm losing it, all grip, all rightness, and I take the tray and go.

John
John would know, would say what needed said, would sit with him, unearth what's bothering, get it up and out. John and him had this knowing between them that I could never. Even though he came out of *me*. Out of me. But John's gone, and that's gone, and maybe that's what this is, although it wasn't a shock, it wasn't sudden, John passing out of our lives, out of life. We watched it, we talked about it, we cried together, it was The Most Terrible. But it didn't destroy us. I thought we were ok. I thought. But now there he is, under the tree, and I hear a sound and I think it's something ripping, something unravelling.

Fivedayssixdayssevendays
My mind's gone on holiday. I'm Robot Mum, preparing food, serving food, lips moving, brain frozen. He's under the tree, still under, still the tree, and trains of thought are barrelling at top speed, carving ravines through me, losing, loss, empty, gone. I'm Pleading Mum now, almost on her knees, whiny-voiced, Why? What are you doing? Please, darling, please, stop this, please please please, and him placid, unmoving, unshakeable. I'm the storm and he is rooted, I try to pull, he

digs even further in, and we are standing still, still standing, sitting, he is, and crumbling, I am.

The Phone

Someone calls, keeps calling, the phone keeps ringing and I keep not-answering because what do I say? Sorry, he can't speak, he's under the tree, yes, in the garden, the tree, been there for a while now, no not hours, days, days, more than one, in the same clothes. What's he doing? Sitting, isn't it? Just sitting, from what I can see, from where I'm standing, shaking, falling.

Ghost

Help me, I say at night, lying in the lonely bed, the marriage bed of not-John and me. Where are you? And there's a whispering in my ear, a shuffling of John-ness, and I know I'm ungripped but I stay with it. It's Duncan, I say, but the John-ness, the -ness of him, knows already, knows about our boy, fixed onto the earth outside. And then there may be words, maybe, justforme words, some sort of sense saying Sit with him, Be with him, Be him, See him, and I'm sleeping and the John-ness is holding on, holding on, until I drift.

Gone

I come down, I stand in the kitchen, I look out, and he's gone. He's gone gone gone, nothing there just grass, rubbing my eyes, stumbling out, insides rising to a spill, but then. No. He's there. A trick, my brain played me, deleting and rearranging, my eyes believed it, my heartsoreness. He's there. There he is. I glide across, sink down, stare into him, drinking him. Still here? I say, Jokey Mum, Shaky Mum, Half-Mum, and he nods, smiles, nods, my Garden Boy, and then his hand is reaching, reaching over to me, for me, gentle and warmly, and I am pulled towards him and I sit, damp on damp grass, with a damp heart bursting, and we sit, under the tree, listening and breathing together as the day begins.

her dirt

She keeps her dirt, and at first her dirt is enough. But then it isn't. So she takes to taking.

There is history here. A clean clean child. Or, rather: demands for a clean clean child. A pure-white home, a childhood washing and re-washing. Do you need to hear of distant mothers and of even further-spinning fathers?

She keeps her dirt in jars, in rows, on shelves, in rooms. She lives, of course, alone. Jars are labelled, jars are all the same. She does not touch the dirt, does not let it glister through her fingertips like stardust. The jars are sealed and left. If asked, she could not say why. But no-one does.

She breaks into her neighbours' homes. She takes her own dustpan and brush and, no matter how many visits from their cleaner, finds something, underneath, behind. She labels, stares and sees no difference: Your dust or mine? His dust or hers?

Then she hears of Arthur Munby. A Victorian gentleman, he was obsessed, it seems, with dirt. Dirty women in particular. Part of her does not want to hear the rest, her insides long ago scrubbed of any thoughts of this. Of what he might want. With them. But when she looks down at her white white arms, her fingernails untouched, unbitten, the pale cloth of her shirt, she feels life spring up inside her.

She goes out for a walk, and at first she doesn't know what she's looking for. She wanders to her nearest train station, and when she is there starts to laugh because she realises she had hoped for coal. But there is no coal, no men kitted out in coal dust, no romantic muscled dark-faced men in this electric age. She will have to go elsewhere.

She takes to walking daily in search of this thing, this idea she could not name if asked, though no-one does. It might be man or woman she is searching for. But everyone is freshly-washed. Even the cats are always cleaning, cleaning.

On one walk, she finds she's left the city. She did not notice, she had been humming to herself. The pavement has ended, she is on a path and by the path hedges are wild, no trimmers here, no neaten-uppers. She is not tired, which is odd, for she has never been that strong. She is not hungry either, although it must have been hours. Her legs keep moving her towards, towards.

The first puddle is a clue and she walks straight through it, no matter shoes or socks or trousers. A second puddle and a third, and she skips through them, off the path now. And then a barn, its door slightly open. Its door inviting.

What does she see when she walks in?

She sees a grey cube, in the middle of the floor. A large cube made of concrete.

She moves nearer and sees that it's not concrete. It's dirt.

She moves even nearer and sees that it's not just dirt. It's *her* dirt. All the childhood dirt she was forbidden. How she knows this she couldn't say if asked, though no-one does.

As she approaches she sees:

- lint from pockets in a favourite summer dress that she was made to pick out with tiny fingers
- mud from their pond that she'd wanted to rub on her face

and arms

- balls of dust from underneath the sofa, where she once hid and sneezed and gave it all away and was dragged out, dust-smeared, and afterwards was hit
- clippings from toenails that were never seen
- clumps of hair from the dog she was not allowed to have
- flakes of her skin from the mattress she cried into when the dog was taken away again

She moves closer still, towards this past-dirt monument. There is no moment when she thinks: How is this here? And: For me? No, there is just her reaching out one arm and then the other, sliding hands into the softness of her-dirt, up to her elbows and then further, to the shoulders, and then she takes that step and walks right in, into the middle of the cube.

As she does, her jars, in rows, on shelves, in rooms, burst open all at once. The dirt – her dirt and his, your dirt and mine – spills out, fountains, spurts, streams and gushes over everything. House dust and grime on every surface, every book, every fork and spoon and knife, every cushion, every shoe and every window sill, until there is a thick thick layer. When it is done, the lids of the jars sigh closed, and everything is blanketed. As if no-one lives here. As if no-one has been here for years, for decades, for millennia. As if we were never here at all.

the angle of his bending

20,000 lead azide detonators could not tear me from you, nor 40,000 caesium-powered rockets, nor 60,000 men with flaming nuclear swords or women with their breasts to tempt me, and he shook his fist into her face as she sat thinking of the space between two chairs which was not enough to keep him from her and the days and days after with no tomorrow to take her away. The rope upon her wrists was tighter now than when he tied it, had some property, she thought, that made it so, and if they had real lives before this all real life was gone. He paced around her now and she tried to see behind him, up and up, but the staircase curved from sight and it was just her in the room with him and rope, and as she saw him bend and stretch she knew the angle a man shudders into with a woman, rope and chairs and all, is never equal to the angles of the opposite sides. And so she stayed silent.

prologue

Just before the novel begins, there is a prologue. The prologue is an entire story to itself. It is the story of the village, before. The village when it was unspoiled, tranquil. The people in the village would fall in love in the fields. A young boy would set his heart on a girl he saw across the wheat, watching as her braids glowed gold in the sun. But it was an innocent love, and they would come together in that same way. And they would say what their hearts felt, say the thing that needs to be said. Before.

And in the prologue there is the story of one such young man, a devoted son, well-loved by his people. He had a job, he worked for the local butcher, and all day he would chop meat, and all day he would serve the women of the village who came for their legs of lamb, their beef, their mutton. He lived with his mother, and she was all that he had, and he was everything to her. On the day she died, young, of a sudden fever, he was inconsolable, and for days afterwards the people of the village, everyday they would keep a watch upon him for they were afraid for his state of mind.

Several weeks passed, and one day he got up and life had returned to him and he began to make order of his mother's belongings. That is when he found the tin full of his mother's letters, and he began to read. He wasn't much practiced in reading, for the people of the village didn't believe in books. Not then, anyway. Not before. He read and he read, and what he read filled him with such a strange emotion, such desires that he could not name. And when he had finished, night had fallen, and he left the house, walked into the fields, lifted up his head and cried out to the heavens.

This is the prologue. And what follows, what the novel is about, comes from this young man, and his cries, his mother's letters. And it tells of how the people of the village never made love in the fields again. Not after what happened.

the watch my father wanted

He reminded me of a sailor, wearing the watch my father had wanted, the watch that my father had made me look at each time we went downtown. Are you a sailor, I said, and he, the sailor with the watch, didn't confirm or deny, didn't smile or stick out a tongue at me, didn't move a muscle. Confused, I walked around him, round and round, and found more things to remind me of my father, my father so long gone and all that pain that drugs could never soothe.

I reached out my hand to touch his shirt, his nautical shirt, I thought, but my hand didn't reach as if there was a wall there, as if there was a logic flying in the face of frontiers and boundaries, barriers and cement fencing. I could keep at you, I said to the sailor with the watch, I could frantically pursue and you would sail and sail and sail and still I would be behind you, and I thought then that the sailor heard me but still he didn't move.

And then I looked to where he was staring, through the window, where the little black dog ran and ran just like the little dog we had when my father. When he was. Where we were and was. Those days I wrote glibly, so happy and so stupid. I was with my father in those days, he and I, we were always, we were like brothers. Then the pain came, and the drugs could not, and the dog was dead. And now I walk past that shop we used to see downtown, and now that watch is gone. I said this to the sailor. Can't buy it for him now, can I? I said. And then I turned my back on him. As I walked away, towards the little black running dog, I thought he spoke. But it was too late. I could not hear him.

ankle socks and hair in bunches

You stand in my doorway with a suitcase.

"I'm here!" you say, smiling so wide I think your face might break. I know you're faking it.

I hope you won't hug me.

I hope you won't even try.

I step back to let you in.

You sit on the sofa. When I bring in the tea, I see us in that 70s home movie. Ankle socks, our hair in bunches, running circles in the garden. You chasing me, me crying.

You look the same. You probably think you have wrinkles, thickened thighs. You probably think the ozone hole has made you leathery. You probably look at me, all skinny, and want that.

You don't want this.

"Alright?" you say, clutching your mug. I force a smile.

"Okay."

Your eyes travel round the room, over photographs and dust and silence.

"I'll do dinner," you say. You go into the kitchen. I stare at your suitcase. I wonder how long you are staying. William strokes my hair. "Shhh," he says, "Don't worry." I close my eyes and listen to you trying to find a pan.

You scramble eggs. I make myself put the fork in my mouth. Then I make myself swallow, because you're watching.

"I'm eating," I say. "Don't worry." I can see your fear, a tight ball. I remember that you love me too.

"A smile!" you say.

"Don't get used to it," I say, egg going down like cardboard. You laugh. You look so much like Mum. The egg starts coming up. I can't make it stop. I run to the loo, bend over the toilet. You aren't laughing any more.

You sleep in William's study. I haven't touched a thing. I stand in the doorway. You pull out the sofa bed yourself. I'm holding clean sheets. I can't remember where they came from. Did I clean them when you'd booked your flight? Were they already washed? Did someone else come in?

I get tangled in these thoughts. You have to nudge me. You have to say, "Here, let me...", take the sheets, make the bed.

I sleep, wake up, go back to sleep, wake up. On and on until it's light. Another day. I hear a noise and think everything's alright. Then I remember.

"Sorry," you say when I come down.

"What for?"

"I dropped something," you say. "I was trying to..."

"I'm not so breakable," I say. I hear William laughing, something about "snapping me like a twig". When I start to cry you dump everything in the sink. We sit at the kitchen table. Me sobbing, and you sobbing too. Because you always did. With me.

Every morning for a week you make me breakfast while I try not to be where I am. Then you try to persuade me to leave the house.

"I'm cold."

"Well, I'll find a sweater, I'm sure you have gloves."

"I'll feel ridiculous. Everyone else in T-shirts."

"Don't be silly." I almost hear you biting your tongue. Of course, that's what I want. For you to lose it. But instead you get gentler. I want to slap you. I hear William saying, "For god's sake, pull yourself together."

Finally, you win. We go out. Me, bundled up and sweating, you propelling me along. I'm paralysed by a row of ants. Or a child on a bike. You have to nudge me into motion. But when we get back, I'm gladder for it, though I don't tell you that.

You make dinner. I lay the table. And then another day is done.

I haven't asked how long you'll stay. I can't see more than five minutes ahead. We make breakfast together now. We listen to the radio.

We go further on our walks. I am not so easily distracted. We can have a conversation.

"Look at that!" you'll say and show me something beautiful. A flower. A dress in a shop window that you won't fit into. Expensive shoes.

You buy chocolate. We sit on a bench and eat it all. A whole box, soft and hard centres. You spit out the orange cream. I laugh.

"Ah, my special trick!" you say. "I have more up my sleeve," and open your mouth wide so I can see the half-chewed caramel. I shove you, you shove me back, but not too hard. 70s home movie. Ankle socks and hair in bunches.

The morning you finally say you have to go, I don't speak. Yes, we go out for walks. No, I don't wake up ten times a night, just five. Yes, I hear William less and less. But. But.

"I think...," you say. "I think you will be ..."

Something is welling up.

"Get back to your life!" I say. "Enough of me, all pale and pathetic. Must have been so shitty for you. What a bloody chore. Just go!"

I am screaming now and then I start to hit you, really punch, not just flailing. My nail catches on your cheek, there's blood, but you don't defend yourself. You're crying, then I am too and we stand, locked together, you holding me so tight that I can't feel any part of me.

70s home movie. Ankle socks and hair in bunches. Sitting on the grass and giggling, Daddy saying, "Into the camera, girls!" We both look at him and grin. Mum calls us in for dinner. You get up first, then pull me up, and we run off together. The garden's empty, only the shapes in the flattened grass say that we were ever there at all.

tiny unborn fish

He brings her to the lab. What does she see? She sees me. She blinks. My timer beeps. She blinks again. I turn, take my test tubes off the rocker. Looking back, he's standing with her, pointing round the room, and she, she's smiling, blinking, smiling.

My hands move without me, flicking open Eppendorfs, taking a pipette. Why's she with him, I want to shake her too. I pick up my protocol. Don't get distracted. Not your business. I look for my solution. Must tidy up my bench. In my head she looks at me and blinks.

We all go to lunch. He's talking, talking, talking. Can't you see that he's moronic? I want to say. She's pale and smiling, opposite me, next to him. He knocks his shoulder into hers. Do you know he's awful, I should say. He gets most of it wrong, he can't think straight, he's got no grasp of anything. Not that we don't all make mistakes, I tell her in my head, as she picks at her sandwich. But there are ones you can't avoid and then there are his, splashing on the bench, like little children flooding sandcastles.

"We're getting married," he says and she looks at me and blinks while he grabs her hand and, like a moron, kisses it. I know I'm on the verge, my eyebrows raising. I stand up, mutter all the things you're supposed to say, and I go.

He brings her to the lab. I turn around and see him leave her there, he rushes off to look important. She's coming this way, my face gets hotter. I motion to a stool. She's moving slowly, as if each lab bench is a minefield, as if her touch might send us up in smoke. She perches, blinking. I peel off my gloves, take new ones from the box.

"Lovely," she says, and her voice isn't high, isn't tentative.

"What?" I say. She nods her head.

"Lovely purple."

I look down at my hands. I never notice anymore. I worry that I'm blushing. I need to speak.

My timer beeps. She laughs and I think that if I could I'd want a timer with that sound, ten or twenty times a day, an hour.

"Your cake ready?" she says, almost a drawl, a wickedness in her look. I grin. She knows that he's a moron. Clearly.

"I'm making scones today," I say, and then we're moving to the microscope room, dark and cool, and she's sitting while I focus.

"Larvae," I say. "Put your head here, can you see them?"

"Little buggers, bloody hell," she murmurs, and I stand beside her in the dark, cool room while in this dish, tiny unborn fish have no idea what's coming next.

the beam line

We had to keep smiling because they spied on us as we queued. If someone let the corners of their mouth droop down, if they let slip even for a second, that was it. A Diamond Light Source uniform would swoop and they'd be gone.

We all had different methods for making sure we appeared cheerful. Some just concentrated on the physical, so that the grin was more of an upward grimace, tiring on the jaw muscles. Others of us decided to think only happy thoughts, let that beam come from within. Easier, perhaps, but who had so many happy thoughts? Hours we waited, and really, if you had that many, why were you here? What did you want?

We didn't know exactly what we were waiting for. We received the invites in the post, everyone in town got one, but all they said was "Find the Secret To Eternal Joy!", the time, the place, and the smiling rule. So we came and stood. The line did move, bit by bit, and the front people did seem to enter the building, but no-one came out that way and so we had no idea what it was all about. There were rumours:

A room shaped liked a hexagon, but with more sides!

Light - light like you'd never seen!

There was a whisper of nirvana, of heights of ecstasy.

We held on to our invitations and we kept grinning as we inched forwards slowly towards it, the destination where we would know it all, where we would finally and totally fly free from the misery of our lives. Those of us who kept our smiles by replaying happier times wondered if we were beginning to feel it already. Small hints, a tiny warmth. Minuscule promises of what was to come.

coat and shoes

Walking in to work from an unfamiliar direction, I saw her, on a street I had never been down before. I was coming from his place, for the first time, after the first time. The first time, but not the first date. That's not me. I'm not one to... not one who... He worked me up to it. Dinners, films. That sort of thing.

So there I was, finding my way along streets I'd only glimpsed, persuading myself that my sense of the office would draw me. And there she was. Sitting on the pavement. Old, I thought. Lost, perhaps. And, as I came nearer, wearing only a nightdress, something thin, flimsy.

Off came my coat and shoes. That's not me, either. Not one to take off my coat outdoors, on a day like that. And shoes? Definitely not. But I looked at her, I took it all in and, without thinking, that's what I did.

I had to dress her. She was limp, like a doll, as I put her arms through the arms and her feet in the shoes. No-one said anything. I dressed her and she stared into the gutter.

When I finished, I almost apologized for that being all I had to give. I mean, I wasn't going to....Wasn't going to hand over my cardigan, my dress, my tights. It was windy. Not cold, or not if you're a person who's used to living in this damp, morbid place. The sun was out, spitting pitiful burns of warmth that ended as soon as they began.

"Do you...?" I asked her, the woman, still staring into the gutter, wearing my coat and shoes. "Your home.. is it...?"

She looked up at me. And I saw that now she wanted to know me, but I didn't say anything. She had my coat and shoes, wasn't that enough? I shook my head. She kept my gaze for another moment and then she dropped hers down again.

I stood for a minute, shifting from foot to foot, and then I raised my hand as if waving, raised it in a half-wave, then dropped it, foolish. Turned around and walked away. I didn't look back. I walked to my office without shoes, thinking of nothing except avoiding what you've got to be careful of on the pavements, what's left to be stepped on.

When I got there, to the office, I went into the toilets, shut myself in a cubicle. Would someone find her? Are they looking? And when they find her, when they help her back home, will they see that the coat and shoes... the coat and shoes aren't hers? What will they say? Will they say, "How strange. Someone dressed her. And whoever dressed her left her there like that." And will they think badly of me?

And if I told *him*? If I called him now, after our first night, what would he say to me? Would he say, "You should have... How could you...?" Or would he say, "Without shoes....You walked all that way...?" And if he said one thing and not the other, what would I say? If he said one thing, and not the other, what would I do?

my flickering self

I stand under the street lamp, my flickering self lit up by doubt and lit up by the lamp and by the moon. I wait under that street lamp for you, all the while vibrations inside me filling me with questions. And you, where are you? Untethered, floating away, leaving me, a stranded star, to shimmer and blister on dark street corners alone. I wait for you to rush up to me, but where you should be rushing there is only silence and where your feet should be there is a cat, moon-widened eyes, afraid to cross *my* path, a witness to my inner ache.

The next day and the next I imagine that street lamp and the rushing of you towards me and the longing in me would fill white bowls full to the brim and overspilling. You do not call. You do not explain yourself, and so I insist that I am still of some use to you by waiting here. I sit in my living room and there is the phone, to hand, by my side, if I can be of use, and I am longing and filling up the bowls.

Finally, a god speaks to you, it seems, and you arrive on my doorstep.

I don't know why you waited, you say to me, a hat on your head but half-falling, and you inside a raincoat, wrapped tight. I told you not to, you said. I told you, and the disappointment is too much for me and I shuffle backwards, back towards my seat and the phone, on whose other end you would have been safer, less poisonous. I sit and watch as you march around and around, lifting and dropping my things, the pieces and bits I have collected, that make me. As you drop each piece, each bit, wrongly, sadly, I don't get up. I resist. I borrow stillness and wisdom from the ancient pine tree and it is only when you leave, your hat still on your head, your raincoat wrapping you tightly, that I lock the door three times, and begin to put all the pieces back in order.

retreating, I retreated

I went down to greet our friends who stood in the drive, stood by the car, stood waiting to be greeted. I thought about the manner of my greeting of them, everyone thinks they are so kindhearted in themselves, everyone believes they will just genuinely be able to welcome, freely and with no conditions. Do you doubt that because I do. I doubt it in myself. As I took a step towards my friends and was seconds nearer to the greeting I doubted very much my ability. But I know that the more you force it to unwind, the tighter it stays rolled up, and so I made to not force anything in myself, I made to shake my arms and legs, to let me loosen as I approached the greeting. I am not much for outings in daylight, but sometimes go out at night in springtime with a large sack, carrying a weight upon me which helps to balance out the air around. I like to have the sack, the weight, otherwise I feel almost falling, almost flying. As I neared the greeting point I missed that, I knew that all could knock me over anytime, the greet might fail, and without the burden to carry what could I put down? How could I look them in the eyes, how could I welcome, how was it possible? And quickly, because the day was chilly, I saw that it was not and started moving backwards. Retreating, I retreated and saw their puzzlement, saw their shock at not been greeted the way a society expects. When I was just far enough away to make it clear but still near enough to see, I saw them getting back into the car. I couldn't make out their faces anymore, I was almost at my door, but

I waved. I waved and knew they wouldn't understand. But I had to wave, I had to do it, it wasn't forced, it was elemental. Then I turned around and went inside.

let's toast this thing

They raised their glasses. Let's toast this thing, they said. Outside it snowed and they did not know it yet but they would not make it home that night.

Other things they did not yet know:

1. The red-haired biologist would be the first of them to die. She would go some years later, in an incident unrelated to her work, on how wounds heal in zebrafish. There would be a red car involved, and the sight of it, the red of the car and the red of the biologist's hair, would cause a person passing by to vomit violently on the pavement and then to feel ashamed.

2. The small woman, brought by the man accepted as the leader of their group, would some weeks later on sit up in bed, while he was still asleep, and not know where she was or why. She would sit like that for several minutes, in half-light, and think sudden thoughts about her mother, long gone and fierce as toast, and, sudden again, would cry.

3. The book that one of them had bought some years before, poetry on Irish lighthouses, a forgettable collection with much simile, much imagery, no heart or guts, would fetch a mint at auction in Dublin. Its value would be increased out of all believing due to the bloody thumb print on page 29 beside the line "she was never to me the same as then, I wept".

4. Several coffee beans which had been roasted in a small African village and which allowed the farmer to send his eldest son to school, would remain behind the stove until the house is bought by new owners. The farmer's eldest son will travel to America and decide to become an actor, which will work out very well for him and land him a role in the blockbuster movie of that year. The new owners will tear out the kitchen, knock down so many walls to "open" it up, and modernise completely, and they will stand in the opened up and modern space and breathe it in and say, Ah, Irish air!, for they themselves are not from here, and then they will bring furniture from France and fill it up until not a space is left to breathe in.

the lion and the meteorite can never touch you

I'll keep you safe, my love, my baby, she whispered into the child's ear, I will never leave you, and the child took it for granted that this was how it would always be. The child grew taller, cleverer, bolder, knowing always that her mother was beside her, ready to throw herself between her daughter and the lion waiting to pounce, the car swerving from its path, the meteorite on its way earthwards. The mother, for her part, did everything her strength allowed to protect the child from any hint of the world as it really is. She sheltered her daughter from tales of rape, mutilation, torture, disease, war and famine. They had no television, the radio was rarely switched on, the atmosphere was peaceful, joyous. The daughter heard nothing of the horrors that we conjur up against one another; she basked in her mother's sun and never doubted her own power.

When they discovered the lump, the mother whispered in her ear as the daughter sat in her hospital bed: You'll be fine, nothing can touch you. The daughter believed her, heard the mother's words as the anaesthetic slid into her veins. When they opened her up and discovered a body with cancer colouring every organ, reaching its insidious fingers into each crevice, encouraging every cell to mutiny, the mother broke down. Doubled over in pain, she screamed at the doctors, losing her sanity because she too had believed what she had whispered.

Come, come, said the daughter, helping her mother into the chair beside her bed. I'm alright, I don't mind it. She felt nothing, cocooned by the medication. But her mother couldn't accept. Her own pains grew stronger and stronger, until she was given her own bed in another ward. The daughter, her suffering body allowing her only to slowly limp along corridors, sat beside her mother, whose pale face was fading with the hours. Thank you, the daughter said into her mother's ear. I'm ready for this. I'm ready for anything. And she watched as her mother broke her promise and left this world. I'm alone now, the daughter whispered to herself, and she closed her eyes and let the disease take hold of her until she, too, slipped away.

the tragedy of tragic men

This is the time of the tragic man, not the drifting cloud. This is the time for all tragic men to come to our aid and for drifting clouds to just move on, move on. They stood in a line to shake his hand, the first and most successful tragic man. But when they came to him, when they stretched out, only air was left within their arms. What a tragic man he is! they said and were satisfied that he was the correct one. The line moved on and on and only one person left morose and ugly. I wish I was tragic too, thought this person, but she was not. Not enough. In a dim age of water she would have floated and that doesn't make for tragedy.

We saw her pass and we got a suitcase and some smaller bags and followed her, the almost-tragic woman, and she noticed that we were there. What? she said and she was angry and we stood in line to shake her hand. What? she said and took our hands and held them and her hands were so soft as if she had no roots beneath the oil paint, she was just puff and cloud. What, she said again and this time she allowed for us to come. And inside we sat and thought about the tragedy of tragic men.

missy

If I had a daughter, this it how it would be. It would be all, *Stand up straight, missy, shoulders back, no slouching*, and she'd be sulky, sullen, pouting, wilful, and I'd see in her eyes, which would be my eyes, that she was starting to hate me, and I'd pour it on thicker. *Smile for the camera, you stupid girl*, I'd be, and, *the lens won't crack, it's seen faces like yours before.* And she'd harbour murderous thoughts inside her little head, shaped like my head, and she'd let her hair, my hair, grow long and unbrushed, and I'd take her and shake her and tell her she'd never amount to anything and she'd hold back from crying, I'd see it in her eyes, my eyes, and I'd see the hate and I'd keep on and on until she left me. On the day she left, I'd be *Fine, then, go out into the world, let's see what you make of yourself, missy, let's see how well you do*, and she'd be sulky, sullen, pouting, wilful, but taller, taller than me, with my eyes, and my hair, and my head-shape, and she'd go, she'd take her things, stuffed into my old suitcase, and I'd watch her back as she walked away without turning round. Then I'd be, *That's right, missy, you go off and you don't think of me*, only I'd whisper this to myself, and, *You live your life the way you want to, not the way I want you to. You be free*, and I'd go back into the house, sit on my sofa, sit quietly, and know I'd done what I needed to do.

we watched him on our screens

We locked him in the Room and then we watched him on our screens. He skipped across the carpet, put his nose up to the window. An airplane flew by and we imagined what he must be thinking. "Freedom?" we wrote in our notebooks. "Or: murder at 10,000ft?" He stayed there for a while then turned and saw the telephone. We had placed it with great care. He slid towards it, extended his left foot, and kicked and kicked and kicked until it fell apart. We looked at one another, nodded, smiled. "Extreme aggression," we wrote down. "Unwarranted and unprovoked."

We took him out to make one small adjustment. Then we put him back and watched. At first he didn't seem to notice. He slipped around the walls, tap-tapping on them with his skinny fingers. But then he marched towards the picture, eyelids flicking. We held our breaths. When he stuck out his tongue, we dropped our pens. And when he licked, up one side of the frame and down the other, we all turned to our shrink. "Impacted neurons?" said our shrink. "Malnourished? Oral fixation?"

We took him out again, made one more adjustment, put him back. This time he saw it straight away. We'd put them in the corner, the little balls of fluff. They were playing, as all kittens do. He stood quite still, his fingers beating out a rhythm on his thighs. We held our breaths. We gripped our pens and notebooks. When he began to cry, to wail and moan, sinking down onto the carpet, we turned again towards our shrink. Our shrink's mouth was hanging open. We wrote something in our notebooks, but couldn't read it later. And still he cried and wailed and moaned. We watched and watched, for twenty minutes, forty seven seconds.

Then he stopped. He stopped as if he'd never cried at all. Then he looked straight at us. And he winked.

We were in uproar! Our cameras were the latest, the very latest thing, made out of the wallpaper itself, how could he possibly? We dropped our pens, our notebooks, cups of coffee. We turned to our technician. Our technician wouldn't meet our eyes. He just stared at his many screens and mumbled gibberish.

We pressed firmly on the buzzer. They came into the Room and dragged him out. We mopped up our coffee; we made sure, with shaking hands, our notebooks were unstained. When he was safely gone, we went into the Room ourselves. We sat down on the carpet, looked around us, then got down on hands and knees and crawled towards the kittens. We played with the kittens for some time. To calm us down, relax us, help us to take stock. Kittens are so useful for that purpose.

acknowledgements

I always turn to the Acknowledgements page of a book first, there's something delicious about it, like peeking behind the curtain in the Wizard of Oz – this is how the wizardry gets done! And it also demonstrates that a book is not about one person, it is the product of so much more than that, and this is my paltry attempt at thanking all those who got us – me and my fictions – to where we are now, to an Acknowledgements page in a book of fictions.

First, my deepest gratitude to all the editors of the literary magazines in whom many of these stories first appeared. Most of you do this for love, with no thought of profit. You gave me the confidence to carry on, without which I am not sure this book would be here. Thank you to BBC Radio 4 who took the "risk" and broadcast eleven of these fictions in the Afternoon Reading programme in June/July 2010, and thank you to Jeremy Osbourne and Sweet Talk for persuading them to and for recording them so beautifully.

Thank you to the members of the Fiction Workhouse (as was), the WriteWords Flash One group and the Zoetrope Flash Factory, the Writers' Round Table, and both writing groups in Israel, where many, many of these stories were written. Thank you to Jon Keating, Dean of Science at Bristol University, for welcoming me in as writer-in-residence. Thank you to Paul Martin and Kate Nobes at Bristol University for allowing me to spend time in your wonderful laboratory, and to Becky, Mathieu, Yi, Will, Rob, Debi, Jenny, Lucy, Jono, Yutaka and Nicole for not minding me staring at you and asking silly questions while you worked. Thank you to Hawthorden Castle, Edinburgh, for the generosity of your fellowship and your hospitality, and to Sue Booth-Forbes and her Anam Cara Writers and Artists Retreat, Beara, Ireland, both magical places which nurture the writer and her imagination.

Thank you to my writer friends, for your support of me and my work, for the conversations/rants about writing, and for being a constant inspiration: Vanessa Gebbie, Carys Davies, Elizabeth Baines, Sue Guiney, Dina Kraft, Devorah Blachor, Lisa Kaufman, Ilene Prusher, Batnadiv Hakarmi-Weinberg, Nadia Jacobson, Aloma Halter, Debora Siegel, Noga Tarnopolsky, Leeora Rabinowitz, Yael Unterman, Sarah Hilary, Elaine Chiew, Susannah Cherry, Sara Crowley, Melissa Lee-Houghton, Michele Tandoc-Pichereau, Margot Stedman, Emma Martin, Sarah Salway, Nuala Ní Chonchúir, David Gaffney,

Marjorie Celona, Evan Fallenberg, Ilana Teitelbaum, Adam Marek, Alison MacLeod, Diane Becker, Clare Grant, Annie Clarkson, Lauri Kubuitsile, Pippa Goldschmidt, Kirsty Logan, Thank you to Jen Hamilton-Emery for making my dream come true and making me an author. Thank you to all my dedicated and hard-working reviewers at The Short Review, and all the Short Review authors, for sharing your words with me and showing me the many things a short story can be.

Thank you to Joe Melia, so much more than "just" the organiser of the Bristol Short Story Prize, Richard Jones of Tangent Books, Joe Burt and Tom Berry, without whom this book most definitely would not exist, especially in its beautiful physical form.

Thank you to my mother, my dad, my stepmother and my brother, for reading my stories and saying that you enjoyed them, even if you weren't sure what they were about!

Thank you to Zachary and Cleo (rest in peace), for being the best writerly cats I could wish for.